# The Cloak of Humility

*Success is Walking Humbly with God*

J. M. Eckert

iUniverse, Inc.
New York   Bloomington

*iUniverse books may be ordered through booksellers or by contacting:*

*iUniverse*
*1663 Liberty Drive*
*Bloomington, IN 47403*
*www.iuniverse.com*
*1-800-Authors (1-800-288-4677)*



*ISBN: 978-1-4401-9587-7 (sc)*
*ISBN: 978-1-4401-9588-4 (ebook)*
*ISBN: 978-1-4401-9591-4 (dj)*

*Printed in the United States of America*

*iUniverse rev. date: 11/23/2009*

I dedicate this book to my children who were the only ones who stood beside me and were loyal no matter what situation I was in. They never left me abandoned and encouraged me to be whatever God wanted me to be. They loved me through every trial in my life and were the wind beneath my wings.

# Contents

# Prologue

The door closed quietly behind her as she stepped outside. The cool breeze felt good as she sat down in the old rocker she had sat in so many times before. As the quiet engulfed her, she began listening to her heart that always told her life's deepest secrets. It seemed as if the quiet lasted forever but suddenly she heard the voice inside that was familiar to her lately.

*"It's almost time to go home now. Do you want to review the road you have traveled through life?"*

She knew what that journey would bring and hesitated for a few minutes. When she went through that door it meant pain and suffering mixed with joy. It also meant repenting and forgiving everyone who had hurt her and those she had hurt along the way.

*"All of the pain and battle scars have become beauty marks in your life. They became victories to me because you grew in my care. Was it not worth it if someone saw me in the midst of your struggles and their life was changed? Wasn't I always there and held you when times were rough? Didn't I always bring the rainbow after every storm and hold you in my arms?"*

A tiny tear slid silently down her cheek and she bowed her head. She suddenly realized that her life had been a journey that led to her heavenly home. Instantly she felt ashamed of the many times she had prayed for material things instead of asking to touch someone's life to honor her heavenly father.

*"I have been here all of the time. I have told you that when you seek me you will find me but the times you couldn't find me were when you were asking instead of seeking. I have chased you all of your life and now it is time for you to chase me. You will find me where I have always been - in your heart. I am your very heartbeat and I will never leave you. I never show myself until you seek me. When you come into my presence I am your covering and nothing can touch you. That is why you must seek me. When you are still in my presence you will know that I am God and I will withhold no good thing from you."*

She bent down by the old rocking chair and lowered her head in reverence to the One who had been her everything for most of her life. She felt the beautiful presence of His peace and knew there was no other place she would rather be. She knew she must start from the beginning when her name was Bonnie because somewhere in the midst of all of her journey she knew she would find treasures she had never seen before.

# A Chosen Child

The day began without a hint of the insignificant event that would change the destiny of the world over fifty years later. There was no warning, and no explanation of why the accident of a small child would ever make a difference in the world. She was unknown and unknowing of God's plan for her life. It was time for the event and thousands of angels lined up to witness the hand of God touch a small child's life.

It was a beautiful day. The wind blew softly in the air and the birds chirped happily in the trees. Bonnie ran down the steps of the house and began chasing Bullet, her shaggy old dog. She was excited because she was three years old today and she would celebrate with Bullet.

Bullet came up and gave Bonnie a big, slurping kiss right on the mouth. This was his gift to Bonnie on her birthday. After all, being three years old today was a big event in a tiny girl's life. If she was good she knew she would get homemade ice cream and maybe even a Coke to drink.

As Bonnie began chasing Bullet around the yard she ran faster and faster. She almost caught him when suddenly she tripped and fell to the ground. It hurt so bad she could hardly talk but she managed to cry for help to her mother. She could not move her leg as she tried to get up.

Minutes later Dr Baize showed up at the house and sat Bonnie on his knee. She kept looking at his little black bag hoping he would have something to fix her leg. Instead, he told her she would have to go to San Antonio where the big hospital was located. They would be able to fix her leg just like new and it would not hurt any more. This sounded like a good idea if they could make her like new but she really wanted the pain to stop at least for a few minutes.

Before she knew it, she was in the old car waiting to have someone stop the pain. At the hospital, they rushed her into a room and took big pictures of her leg. She thought to herself that they should be making her leg all right instead of taking pictures but grown-ups sometimes seem to do strange things.

The next thing Bonnie knew she was on a big table with a bright light shining in her face. Someone put a mask over her mouth and as she struggled to move everything went black. When she woke up she was in a bed and her leg was tied up in the air. The pain was terrible as she lay there being unable to move. She began crying as she thought about the beautiful birthday that she never had the chance to finish. The ice cream she had wanted so much seemed unimportant now and there was nothing to celebrate. She silently wondered when she could go home and chase Bullet again. Next time she wouldn't fall because she wouldn't get on the sidewalk.

It seemed years but finally the day came when her mother and dad loaded her into the old car and they started home. She looked down at the cast that went from her waist to her ankle. It was so heavy she could hardly lift it. She just knew that soon the doctor would take it off and she could chase Bullet again.

*"This was your first battle scar. It became the biggest beauty mark in your life, child. I allowed this to happen because I knew the intent of your heart. If I had left you perfect you would have become vain and rejected me. I made you beautiful in every way when you were born. You could have won any beauty contest but it would have been your downfall. I couldn't take the chance of losing you so what Satan meant for your harm I have used for your good. Never again mourn that your body is imperfect because this made your heart soft and tender."*

She looked at the small child she had been so many years ago. The cast on her leg had been so heavy. When she was tired she would climb up in the wheel chair that her parents had gotten for her. It had looked so huge to her. She could barely see the seat she sat in but she knew she could climb up into it by using her good leg. When she sat down she could talk to Bullet and hold him close. Every time she climbed into that big chair Bullet would come and jump into her lap. He was her best friend and she would hold him close as she told him about her day. Bullet was always so polite and he would listen as long as she talked to him. Sometimes he would lick her hand as if to agree with what she said. Then he would lay his head on her cast as if to sympathize with her.

*"Did you know that I was touching you through Bullet? I heard every word you said and I held you every day. I love my children through many different sources. When Bullet looked at you it was really my eyes that saw your pain and suffering. You have always been my daughter and my hand has been upon your life. I was the soft wind that blew your hair and cooled your body when it was hot. I flew all around you in the butterflies and watched you during the day. In fact, I was everything around you and I placed a covering of protection around your life that has never been removed. That is how much I love you."*

It was then she realized He had been with her all of her life. She had always thought that God was only there when she prayed. If only she had known this from the beginning she would have walked in faith like it says in His word. Then she understood that even when she didn't pray He had led her on the path that had been designed uniquely for her life. It didn't matter that she was just now learning His awesome power because He had directed her life by his spirit and mercy. He always took the measure of faith she had used and touched her life time and time again. What a loving God he truly was. The eyes of her understanding had begun to open and suddenly she was excited to learn more about the One who had been with her all the days of her life. It no longer mattered that she had gone through her life with a crippled leg that was covered in scars.

The simple break to her leg became infected from the heavy cast. She had two more operations and huge scars on her leg. The surgeon cut on her leg so many times there was very little muscle left and it grew to the bone, leaving her leg stiff.

*I covered you with the spirit of humility when you received your first battle scar. This first battle in your life would be the greatest beauty mark in your life. There is no greater anointing on my children's life than the character of humility. I can never flow in a person's life to walk with them daily unless they are humble to me. Through humility comes obedience and this allows me to be the Master of your life. It is then that I can be your strength in times of weakness. I can guide you along the road of life and display my glory. It is my glory that sets the captives free and brings victory. When you told Bullet your leg hurt I heard you. Satan had plans to take your leg but I took you to the hospital and stopped the infection. I bore your pain again and held you close through it all. I allowed the pain to produce a greater beauty mark. Satan would always try to destroy you because I loved you so much and He would bring pain to you at every chance. The pain brings strength and faith, which was my special gift to you. I can turn anything that Satan means for your harm into something good. I had great work for you to do and the final step was to write this message. Through your suffering I caused compassion for others to know the fullness of my being. When your destiny is completed I will tell you well done my child.*

*I added a special gift to your life. It was favor wherever you went. Sometimes you saw it and sometimes you didn't recognize it at the time. As we continue to take this journey you will see it and know that I was there all of the time."*

Her wrinkled face smiled as she realized His great love. Suddenly every wrinkle was cherished because they were really beauty marks from the battle scars of her life. She thought about all of the women that rushed to the doctor at the sign of age. They would do anything to remove those beauty marks. They did not know that they were really marks of victory that God had won. They were removing precious gifts their heavenly Father had so carefully given to them. No wonder her Father wanted her to review her life and tell others. Her eyes had been opened and she must share the truth with anyone who would listen. For years He had asked her to write to others but there had many so many excuses. She didn't have enough time and then she had no computer. Imagine that.

She had grown up without computers in existence and her time had belonged to Him. Repentance suddenly consumed her as she whispered, "I'm sorry heavenly Daddy."

*"You were forgiven back then but now you are delivered from the accuser. Do you see now why this journey is important? To enter into my heavenly kingdom I am here to settle every issue that has been in your life. I try to do this with all of my children but many never pay any attention. My word tells you to ask me forgiveness for your sins daily so they don't grow and accumulate over the years. When you ask for forgiveness you need to name your sins. Ask me to show you what each one is so that nothing is overlooked. Sins are caused when humility to me is missing. The cloak of humility is your protection from the luring of the evil one that watches your every move. When you wear the cloak I can flow through you and bring your victory. When your eyes are on me you will never see defeat. Remember this from now on - humility brings faith. Faith wins every battle. It is impossible to please me without faith. I never see your tears until I see your faith. Your faith releases my mercy and*

*causes me to move in your life. Faith causes you to keep your eyes on me and that is when I bring the victory. As we travel the road of your life I will increase your knowledge to absorb the mysteries of my kingdom. All of the ones that read this will receive knowledge so they will learn my ways. My teaching through this will change millions of lives. You must always wear the cloak of humility to accomplish this work through you. I speak to each of my children individually so fear not what I write through your hands. All that receive it and act upon my teaching will be blessed. You have been praying for me to bless you so you would be a blessing to others. My blessing is now upon you to let me speak through your life."*

Quickly she knelt beside the old rocking chair. Her heart's desire was no longer to have riches on earth. Riches in heaven were now waiting for her arrival. She could envision millions that would listen to the Father's teachings and be instantly changed into His likeness. There was no greater time in history this change was needed. Her Father's world was out of control and His heart was crying to help His people. She kneeled quietly as His precious spirit consumed her entire being. What a privilege to service the One who had given her life. He had not only given her life but had loved her so much He would use her for His glory. No wonder Satan had tried to destroy her so many times. If he had taken her life God's mission for her would never had been accomplished. She never wanted to take off the cloak of humility again. It was so ugly to the eyes of the world but it was the most precious thing she had ever worn.

The little girl celebrated her twelfth birthday. That day her best friend arrived and introduced himself. He had been there all of her life but she had never known His purpose in her life. His name was Jesus and He was so wonderful. The aura of His presence brought a new meaning to her life. All of her friends in the past had said hurting things about her. Some had even made fun of her limp when she walked. She knew this new friend would never leave her or forsake her. She asked Him to be her savior and to never leave her. His very presence assured her this friend would be there and never leave. At the time she didn't know just how important He would be in her life. He would teach her what a true friend should be. Later she would learn His ways and allow Him into all of the rooms in her heart.

The first room she and her best friend visited was love. He emptied His enormous blessing of love right into her heart and became the Lover of her soul. That love would carry her all the days of her life and be the spirit of compassion for others. When others mocked and looked down on her she would learn to pray for them. She would know that their actions were caused by their own pain and lack of knowledge. She loved the room that held His love and ran to it continually. His love brought a peace that engulfed every thing in her life. His love gave strength and encouragement and it never condemned her.

*"I have given you my greatest gift. He is the sacrifice for all of your sins. Listen to Him and He will guide you throughout all the days of your life. He suffered more than you will ever realize to become your best friend. He is the only way you can enter my throne room until I bring you home to me. Anything you have need of He will provide for you. I created the rooms in your heart for Him to abide beside you. He will knock on each door in your heart before He enters. Invite Him in to know His fullness. My work in your life will not be completed until each room is filled with my glory. When I begin my work in a child's life I anoint them with a new name. You will now be called Mercy. It is mercy you will need the most to follow me because of your humanness. The world will never call you mercy until they know me personally. I will personally call you Mercy as long as you walk with the new best friend you now have. Treat Him with respect because He is a perfect gentleman. He will be your strength and carry you when you are weary. He will comfort you and be your provider.Share every area of your life with Him and He will never leave you. That is what a best friend does but the world is not capable of being a best friend."*

What an amazing birthday gift her Father had given her. She now had a new best friend and a new name. This meant a new beginning for her life that had been so much suffering. She told her parents and they shared her joy. She was yet to realize that they were the ones that had invited her best friend to meet her. Jesus had quickly introduced Himself to her knowing that He would soon be the replacement of her family. In fact, He would replace everything during her lifetime. This true gentleman that had become her best friend would be her guide and never leave her. It would take most of her life to realize His importance. Every time she saw His greatness she learned to trust Him more.

Mercy grew in the presence of her best friend. Others still made fun of her limp but it didn't hurt any more. Her best friend took the pain and cast it far away from her life. All she had to do is visit the room of His love and tell Him all about her day. He fed her His word a spoonful at a time in the beginning. Each word was a seed He planted in her heart that would be nurtured all of her life. Humility watered and nurtured each word to produce the harvest He had in store for her. He was not concerned how long it would take for the harvest. He would never give up on her until the harvest was complete.

She had her sixteenth birthday. Of course her best friend was there. She never wanted to go anywhere without Him. Soon after she awoke one morning her sister-in-law came in.

"I need to tell you something, my sister. Mother just passed away a few minutes ago."

Mercy didn't understand at first. Her mother had just kissed her goodbye less than an hour ago. She ran to her best friend for comfort.

*"I took her to be with me. She knew that I would take care of you and was ready to come home. Don't be afraid or discouraged. I will always be with you and never leave you. She wouldn't leave until*

*she knew I was in your life. I will take your mother's place now. Rejoice and be glad that she is safe with me now and will never suffer again. She had much suffering in her life because she chose to serve me. She will now receive her reward of a heavenly home. She had many jewels in her crown and one of them was you. I placed each jewel in her crown and no one can remove them. Someday you will understand more but until then just rest in my care."*

Immediately an anointing of peace fell upon Mercy. She stood up and went to her room. She asked her best friend to forgive her for being rude to her mother just days before. Her heart was broken because she had hurt her mother and not asks for forgiveness. She wanted her friend to be sure to tell her mother that she was sorry. She hadn't even told her mother she loved her that morning when came in to kiss her goodbye. She had pretended to be asleep and had not responded. Mercy asked her friend to please forgive her for being so cruel. His peace never left her as she began each new day. She learned that His peace is never ending while in His presence. That peace would be her strength from that day forward.

*"The loss of a mother is always one of the greatest pains of man. Many of My children are closer to their mother than anyone else. When I take her unto myself I take her place in your life. The only greater love than a mother's is mine. That is one of the times my grace is sufficient in your life. I see your repentance of disrespecting your mother and you are truly forgiven. After all of the years it is only now that you are willing to release the guilt to me. When there is repentance Satan rushes in with condemnation and guilt. If you believe him those burdens are added in* your life and become heavy. Until you fully believe you are forgiven and *accept my forgiveness I cannot release those burdens. My forgiveness will now heal you and you are set free. She forgave you the day you asked for forgiveness so does not look back with sorrow again. Your repentance nurtured compassion for my children and your wrong was turned into good by my hand. You must have my compassion for me to touch others though your life. I have taken your tears of repentance and nurtured*

*the seed of compassion in your heart. Rejoice for your shedding of tears. They have been used for my glory."*

Mercy tried to remember back to those last days with her mother. She wondered if she knew she was leaving for heaven and rejoiced. She didn't remember her being sad or even sick. It had been over 44 years since her mother left but she could still remember her smile. There was such sweetness in her countenance and a kindness in her touch.

She knew now that the Master had been with her through her mother during those years. It was His smile and His touch she had known and loved. Her mother had been a chosen one by God. The anointing had been passed from her mother to Mercy when she left. That anointing had brought the peace to her. The journey of life was becoming more vivid and real than she could imagine. Now she was no longer afraid of facing the rest of her travel down the road of life. She was sure of who had held her hand now.

The best day of her life was only two weeks away. Mercy was so excited to get to the cemetery and tell her mother the latest news. When she got there she sat down at her mother's grave. There was so much to tell her and she knew her mother could hear her voice. She told her first that she missed her so much and wished she could be with her. Dad was fine and had met someone that seemed good for him in his loneliness. He had started to smile again since she had left. Then she told her the latest and greatest thing in her life. She had met her soul mate and he was breathtaking. She was deeply in love with him and they would be married in two weeks. Dad seemed to like him and he had nice parents. She was sorry she would not finish her senior year in high school but she had promised Dad she would get her GED. She told her mother that she wished she could meet him but she knew someday she would. Finally, she whispered tearfully that she loved her and missed her more each day. She told her she would see her again when God took her to heaven. Mercy then rose slowly from the ground and walked away. Her best friend walked with her and held her closely to His side. He caught the tears that slid down her cheeks and handed them to their heavenly Father.

*"I took those tears and put them in a tin cup for future use. I knew that during the years to come you would add many more and someday I would use them to wash away the pain of your past. Look at that old tin cup now. It is full and almost overflowing. When we finish our journey I will take the cup of tears and anoint you with them. They will wash you clean and heal you of your past. Each tear has a story. Only I know each story of your life. I walked every step with you. Sometimes I even carried you. The times I carried you were when you thought I wasn't there. You only saw one set of footprints and thought they were yours. I would hold you tight until you felt my presence. You would grab my hand and we would begin walking together again. I carried you* home *that day when you left the cemetery. Then I held you all night and poured my love into your heart. My love gave you the strength and courage to face the years ahead. The storybook romance you thought would be turned out to be a rocky road of trials. My protection never left you and has grown with you during the years. It taught you the power of my resurrection and the deepness of my love."*

Mercy thought about that decision she had made so many years ago and wondered what would have been if she had not married. Then she realized that God had brought many good things from her decision. He had turned something wrong into many things right. She had three children that were His from that relationship. Her mother-in-law had been a mother to her and loved her when she needed a mother's love. She knew her Father had loved her through each person involved in her life. With that thought in mind she whispered "Thank you" and asked forgiveness for not seeking her Father's advice. She could so easily have asked Him to show her the way He had planned for her. Now she understood why He tells His children to not lean on their own understanding. She had looked at the outer appearance of man and not at his heart.

*"It is alright, child. I could have stopped your decision in many different ways. I know my children's life from beginning to end. Although it was not my perfect will I am creative and knew it would be all right. It is going to become rougher as we walk down the path of your life. Keep in mind that every pain you feel was turned into a victory by my hand. When we complete our walk down the road you will rejoice knowing I overcame every obstacle you faced. We better get started again so I can fill you with my joy."*

# The Beginning

*M*ercy was so excited. She just knew life was going to be full of rainbows and sunshine. The one she had met was going to go through life with her just like her parents had done. After all, marriage was supposed to be togetherness. She couldn't remember her parents having problems and she often saw them smiling at each other. Didn't that mean that marriage was wonderful and exciting? They gave her so much love she was certain the world was full of love.

It wasn't long until she experienced the behavior of a person she had never known before. He was full of anger, jealousy, deceit, and had a controlling spirit that almost suffocated her at times. She thought if she tried harder he wouldn't be so upset with her. She had never seen her dad act this way so it must be her fault. She became a victim and never knew what was happening.

The harder Mercy tried the worse things became. He would hit her occasionally and use words she had never heard before. Thank goodness she could always run to her best friend, Jesus. He always held her and filled her with His love.

*"I was there and never left. Many good things came from that union. You learned perseverance. The seed of humility and obedience was planted deep within you as you stayed where you had no place. You followed him all over the United States and had his children. I turned all of the marks on your body into beauty marks. The scars on your heart were deep but I touched them and healed you when you sought me out. You took him to church and I touched his heart but he turned away soon thereafter. I knew I must deliver you from your prison. Your heart had become so fragile it needed a rest. That is when I brought someone else into his life to set you free. It broke my heart every time you would cry for me to bring him back home because I knew he was not ready to change. My grace was sufficient to see you through."*

*"When he left I gave you a beautiful gift which was the life of your son, Casey. Then I bound the hearts of you and your children together for each of you to endure the race of life. You see child, you had looked to him more than you looked to me and I never allow that in my children's lives. I must be first to you and he had taken my place. I held you when he left and knew your healing was just beginning. By My strength you would endure the years ahead and become a shining jewel in my kingdom. Jewels do not shine when first found. They are polished and protected by their owner. I have refined you into pure gold for my kingdom. No one knows your value but me lest they steal you from my arms."*

*"Remember when you were driving and the radiator busted on your legs? It was freezing cold in January and you began crying. You cried all the way home and ran to your room. You asked me to take you home because you were tired of trying. I came into your room and you felt my presence. My presence is strong and you knew I was there. I told you to call a friend and ask them to help you find a car. I picked a special car for you. It was dark red to symbolize the blood I shed for you. I even had the dealership deliver it to you and you cried tears of joy. You thanked me and planted a seed of faith into my ministry. Soon my gift had a bumper sticker on it that*

*read EXPECT A MIRACLE. There would be many miracles ahead and the first one was on the way."*

Mercy knew what the next miracle was. It was the arrival of a child she named Casey that would bring the family joy and unity. He was born in a lowly setting. Mercy had worked two jobs to pay for his birth. When he decided to come she called friends close by. They picked her up and took her to a town near by and dropped her at the front door. Her two older children left with them and she stared at the entrance door in front of her. It was past midnight and she beat on the door with tears streaming down her face. As she entered the hospital she felt His presence and she walked inside. She knew her Master was there and would never leave her. It no longer mattered that she had been left alone. He was all that she needed. When Casey was born she paid the doctor and hospital for his birth. She was so thankful that God had provided the money. Mercy bowed her head and thanked her Father for purchasing her son. She knew he would be another jewel in her crown.

*"Is it too painful to go on right now, child?"*

He took her in his arms and began rocking her gently. He touched the battle scar with His nail-scarred hand and peace surrounded her. In the place of the scar was a huge new beauty mark. It radiated with His glory.

*"The beauty mark I gave you will shine throughout your life. It is my mark of love and it will cause you to witness of my glory many times to come in the future. Everyone in your life will turn his or her back on you at some time in your life. Each time you will learn more about my faithfulness. Each step we take down your road of life will bind our hearts closer together until I bring you home with me. That beauty mark alone has destroyed the seed of pride that you had hidden in a room of your heart. You always boasted that you had survived in life because you were strong. Now you will not forget that you are weak and it is your weakness that brings my*

*strength. It was only a few weeks ago you told someone you did it by yourself but from now on you will profess my strength and not yours. All beauty marks I give are embraced with your humility to me. I have forced you to walk by faith so that the small seed of faith you started with can grow to magnify my greatness. Keep your eyes on me and I will show you how really great I am."*

Mercy looked at her Master and knew she must go on. He had given her a better job after Casey was born. He had even helped her start a new business and it thrived with His favor. She remembered she had asked Him to let her stay home and raise her children so she could teach them His ways. Little did she know what was about to happen. She quit her paying job and soon her business was gone. He answered her prayer and replaced it with self-employment to work when she could. Money was scarce and there was no one to help her. She began reading the Bible and read it from beginning to end many times. During these years she kept praying that God would bring her children's dad back home. God was silent and did not respond.

*"He was not the one to raise my children. I would not allow anger and control into their lives or yours either. I will tell you no if the results of your prayer will bring you harm or lead you on the wrong path. Cherish the word "no" when I speak it to you. You must trust me to make the final decisions in your life. There are always times when you do not understand why I did not answer your prayer and say yes. Now you realize when you prayed with your mind that was not anointed with my wisdom you would have to wait for me to answer. If the request was urgent to you then you would seek me and I would give you wisdom. If you know my word then you know my heart. I need you to teach my children the truths I am teaching you now. Because of your many trials in life you understand where they are and you know that I am the answer. It is not easy to be a chosen child of God but it rewarding above your imagination. You will feel my heart beat and become one with me in the spirit. Once you become one with me you will never want to go back to the way you were before. Trust me in what I am saying to you and there will*

*be roses where the barren thorn bush was in your life. You will hear my voice and I will be so close you will no longer see yourself. My spirit will guide you and then you will no longer ask me what to do because you will know my voice. Before you even ask I will answer and show you the way each day. When you are with someone they will feel my anointing and I will speak through your lips. When they hear your voice or read your words they will feel my presence and they will have hope. Many days in the past you begged me for hope. You now have my anointing that will give you hope. Your hope will help others to know my power. It is my presence that brings my power. Will you trust me to do this in your life?"*

Mercy felt His presence and knew His words were true. She had no desire to return to living without the fullness of His presence. This would require a lot of faith, which would have to come from her Master.

As Mercy sat back down in the old rocker she heard her dad's voice. It was so real and clear she looked to see where it came from. He told her the Master had taken him home that day so long ago. Before he left he had been reassured she would never be alone. Mercy realized that was when she had begun calling her heavenly Father her Daddy. Her dad looked so happy and told her there was nothing like heaven. He and her mom spent their time worshipping at the feet of Jesus and had seen the mansion God had designed just for her. Every detail was designed by the Father's loving hands and was almost ready for her. Every sacrifice she had made for His glory had been placed in that mansion and it was pure gold.

She listened closely as her Father led her further down the road. She stopped and saw the man she had hoped would be a father to her children. He didn't look like she had remembered him. He was gray and old looking with tattered clothes. He walked with a limp and held his head down. He told her that he was sorry he had not been a father to her children. She forgave him for never being there for them. Then she told him to rejoice. He had given her their beautiful daughter and she belonged to God. She was a rare jewel in her crown and priceless. As she looked upon his weary body the forgiveness flooded her being. All resentment and anger from the past fell off and the burden was lifted. He had never been supportive emotionally and gave very little money but she knew her daughter could not be bought with a price. She understood financial poverty but enjoyed spiritual prosperity to the highest degree. She thanked him and told him that both God and she forgave him. She saw the angels surround him and praise God that he had been set free.

*"Did you see the chains fall from his life? When you forgave him you released him from guilt and shame. Few realize the bondage they place on my children's life by harboring unforgiveness. You must share with others the great healing I give when you release someone held by unforgiveness. His guilt was a heavy burden all of these years and brought resentment he held against you. By forgiving him you have been set free, too. The chains of darkness are strong and cause oppression and defeat. It is my spirit within you that forgives and forgets. You can now respect him as the father of your daughter. "*

*"Do you remember when the two of you prayed for him to quit drinking and sent an offering to one of my servants? I honored that offering and request and I delivered him from alcohol in three days. You didn't stand by him after that but I forgave you. He knows me now and listens to my voice. I hear your request to be forgiven and I will tell him now. I will help him to forgive you for abandoning him in his time of need. I declare you both healed of your past and I set you free."*

She was beginning to realize there had been many chains of bondage on her life. Now she understood why it was so important to take this walk with her Father. Each battle in her past would be completed with victory from her Father's healing hands. All of these years she had only looked at her own chains of bondage. Now she saw that the bondage she had placed on others lives had placed those chains on her. She couldn't change the past but she could let her Master be in control of her future. So many times she had blamed others for everything that was wrong. She had been a victim of the "poor me" syndrome and never looked upon her own faults.

The cloak of humility was comforting now. Mercy knew that as long as she wore the cloak she would stay in her Father's arms.

As he led her forward in their walk together she saw her dad. She had lost him when Ashley was only one year old. His face was glowing and he looked radiant. She had missed him so much during all of the years. He had been her hero. When she had lost him there was no one on earth to run to anymore. Her mother was standing by his side and their joy engulfed her being. He whispered he loved her and told her they would be waiting when it was time for her to come home.

*"I became your Daddy when I brought him home to me. At that time you had to start leaning on me alone. You have wondered all these years why you never received your inheritance from your parents. They gave you the inheritance of heaven and that was more important. Satan may have taken your material inheritance but he knew he couldn't take you from me. You didn't know at the time that I carried you more than you walked for a while. You were weak and I filled you with my strength. You called his leaving a loss but it was so much more. He was united with the wife of his youth and he left all pain behind when he left. Before he came home he asked me to never leave you. He wanted me to take his place in your life and I have done that through all of the years. As I carried you I would always whisper that I loved you. I have been your comfort and constant companion since that time."*

Mercy was beginning to realize her Daddy's awesome power. She clutched the cloak of humility tightly and whispered thanks to the One who had never left her. She was so thankful that He had given her parents that were His chosen children. The beauty of His presence made her wonder how her stepmother had misunderstood her and said horrible things about her. She asked her Daddy why her stepmother had attacked her verbally so many times to others during the years after her dad had died. Maybe there was something she had done and needed to repent of her actions. This lingering hurt needed to be resolved now.

*"You were the apple of your dad's eyes. Every time your name was even mentioned his eyes would light up and a tiny smile would appear on his face. He would sit for hours waiting for your phone call and many times it never came. When you came to see him you would sit with him in unity as you discussed your life with him. There was such a strong bond between the two of you and the stepmother resented it. She thought you disrespected him by not calling or coming to see him often. She never understood how your hearts were bound together and how you both knew each other's love. She told everyone that would listen that you was after his money and didn't care about him. The bond that you had with him was threatening and made her feel insecure. That insecurity became a poison in her heart and it erupted at his death. He had taken good care of her children but the bond was not there. The son they had together was his other bond and those bonds with his natural children became more than she could understand. When your dad died it was the opportune time for Satan to begin his final attack through her lips. She decided you would receive nothing but a few tokens left from your dad's life. I protected you from many of the arrows that Satan aimed at your life because I knew that someday you could receive the truth about her. It is time for you to forgive her now. When you do you will release her chains of resentment and set her free. I have protected you from all of the negative words spoken against you that you never knew about. Let it go now so a beauty mark can be placed on the scars of that battle field."*

Mercy bowed down by the old rocking chair. The tears began flowing and she couldn't stop them. Her body began to shake with emotion as her Daddy's presence covered her. She asked forgiveness for not spending more time with her dad while she had him. Then she repented of the hurt and resentment she had felt against her stepmother for twenty-two years. She asked her Daddy to bless her stepmother and set them both free from the past. Although she still didn't understand why she was refused the few things belonging to her mother and her maternal grandmother she didn't want to know why anymore. Those material things could never be recovered so she knew she must let go of the loss.

*"She kept those things because she thought you were selfish and wanted them for their value. She was the one that wanted them because she loved antiques. The sentimental value they held for you never entered her mind. She also knew how much your dad loved your mother and felt inferior to that love. I have to tell you these things so that the seed of not knowing will never enter your mind again. The treasures lost on earth are much less than the treasures I have for you with me. I have replaced those lost treasures many times over and have them waiting for you to see. The greatest treasures are spiritual and you are experiencing their value now. Very few of my children learn this during their* lifetime *because they do not seek me with all of their heart. Rejoice at the loss of the small material things and know they brought you another beauty mark from their scars. What Satan meant for your harm I have turned into something good in your life? The chains of bondage from your past are being removed one by one. Are you ready to remove some more chains in your life?"*

The healing that was taking place in Mercy's life encouraged her to move forward in their journey. First, she lifted her hands in praise to her Healer. She was just beginning to realize just how much He loved her and she cherished His love. He had cared about the smallest of things and she had not known it at the time. The false accusations of her stepmother had been stopped before they had ever reached her ears. She had felt their arrows close by but they had never pierced her heart. Now she began to understand why her Daddy had said there is the power of life and death in the words you speak. Words can destroy relationships and consume a person's hope until they are so weak they give up trying. Satan takes wrong thinking he has placed in our minds and develops those thoughts into fiery arrows of accusations. She was now seeing that the only way to have the character of Christ was to spend time in His presence and teach His ways. His spirit covers the heart and makes it pure like His. That is why He told us that love covers a multitude of sins. She seldom remembered that His greatest commandment was love. Now she understood why it was so important. Her Daddy was total love and that love had protected her from the accusations spoken against her. In fact, He had loved her so much many accusations spoken against her had never reached her ears. His kindness surpassed her understanding because she knew she didn't deserve a love that great. It was her dad's love expanded many times over and it consumed her entire being. This walk they were taking together through life was changing her moment by moment and she was leaving the past behind.

*"I want you to understand why we are spending a lot of time in this area of your life. The years you were learning to serve me and the effect others had in your life has brought you to this place. You picked up habits and prejudices that need to be removed. Wrong thinking and actions are copied from your heroes in childhood and become stronger as you grow older. The most important request you ever made to me was for me to be a father to your children. Even though you did things wrong I covered them and made those things right in their lives. I gave them a special wisdom to see the good and reject those things of the evil one. When they did partake of things of the world I convicted their hearts and they knew it was wrong. My spirit and protection has never left them from the day you asked me to be their father. I took that request seriously and never left their side. It was my spirit that prompted you to pray that prayer because I knew you would serve me."*

Mercy realized she was receiving fruit of the spirit of God and it was filling. She thanked her Daddy for everything He had allowed in her life. Each detail had worked for her good to mature in His ways. She knew He had given her a caring heart for His children. Compassion flowed from her toward others and many times when she saw someone in need she would cry tears of compassion for that person. She had a longing desire to help others and this walk would prepare her to be strong and wise. No longer did she have any desire to blame others for her own mistakes. The cloak of humility was cleansing her of her past and all wrong thinking. Poverty and lack no longer seemed as important as trusting God as her provider. She had asked Him to be her husband and He was the perfect model. An earthly husband could never come close to His greatness and care. All of the burdens of her past continued to vanish as she sat in His presence. She wanted to be set free completely and begin serving Him with her cloak of humility clutched tightly around her body.

The children seemed to be growing so quickly and Mercy still had the longing for an earthly father to be involved in her children's lives. The two oldest had already left home but the two younger ones had never had a male authority to shape their lives. Another man entered their lives at this time. He said that he was a Christian and that seemed good enough for the situation. She didn't ask her Daddy's approval. In fact, she didn't even discuss the matter with Him. The man entered their lives and gave Casey and Ashley attention they needed so much. However, Satan covered him and pursued her everywhere she went and in everything she did. It belittled her and was an accuser of her spirit. In the meantime Casey developed a relationship with the man causing Mercy to wonder what to do. She prayed and asked her Daddy for answers and he answered her in the midst of the storm.

*"I did not answer for the purpose of condemning you. I answered to deliver you. When you asked me to help you was the first time you had given me permission to move in your life. I looked upon each person involved to assess the damage. You did not even see the spirit of manipulation that had set in on your family. I had to terminate the relationship to bring spiritual health back to each one of you. You had forgotten my teaching that the family that*

*prays together will stay together because I am the teacher. You ran and Satan pursued you. I was still the heavenly Father to Casey and Ashley and I knew how to turn those scars of life into a beauty mark for each one of them. You did wrong by replacing him with someone you thought would be a better father. I counseled you but you didn't listen to my warnings. That relationship was filled with resentment of your children. The man was covered with greed, selfishness, and had an inferior complex. Resentment controlled the family and destruction was near. In all of your faults his older son saw your faith in God. It gave him hope and I claimed that son for my glory. You see that I made beauty marks out of many scars in that relationship. Then you realized I was the only one that could be the Father your children needed. Your search was ended and you surrendered to me completely."*

Mercy was ashamed she had not listened to her Daddy. She knew He had tried to show her the way to go. She asked Him to forgive her for her wrongs to the ones she had chosen to be a part of her life. Then she asked him to take the scars she had made in their lives and replace with beauty marks from His hands. At that moment she felt a release from her guilt and shame. She saw the chains falling from her and their bondage vanished. Never again would she look back with sorrow of her decisions. Now she is thankful for her freedom she had been given. She fell prostrate on the floor and whispered "I love you" to the One who had redeemed her and set her free. The hidden room in her heart that had been filled with resentment and unforgiveness was instantly filled with His love. His love brought a peace so strong she rested quietly in His arms.

*"We have gotten past the replacements of me in your life now. We can review your life and walk the rest of the way together without division. Do you understand now why we had to start from the beginning? Each room of your heart had to be cleansed and filled with me. I will give you a fresh new filling of my spirit each day as you come to me in prayer. That is why I desire my children to come to me when they rise each day. You can start the day with me and*

*be covered by my spirit to protect you. Instead of running to me when there is a problem you will have my strength to confront each problem as it appears. My spirit gives you the wisdom to make the right decisions and avoid disruptions in our relationship. We have settled all relationships of your past and can decide how to guide your children now. Listen at all times for my instruction because it will prevent any stumbling blocks in their life. I will anoint you now as a counselor to your children that has my anointing and wisdom. As you become obedient to my voice I will give you compassion for other children that I will bring into your path. You must be ready to receive them and feed them with my teachings for my teachers are few. I am trying to claim all of my children so that I can deliver them into my kingdom. My words are life and I will place life upon your lips."*

# The Oldest Son

She knew she must begin with the oldest child. God had shown her the destiny He had given her son and she knew he had God's favor. He was blessed with many talents. It was apparent from the beginning he would be a leader and greatly used by the Master. He was given a tender heart to have compassion for others. She understood why his earthly father was removed during his childhood. It was the only way the heavenly Father could train this son in the way he was to go. He was named Justin and a cousin spoke words of wisdom over his life when he was born. He said this tiny child looked like a judge and began calling him the judge. It was at that time that Mercy knew the Father would use this child to be a righteous judge for His other children.

*"I took the rebellion caused by the pain in his life and turned it into compassion. Every disappointment he had was used to help others. The loss of his dad in his life helped him to relate to all of the fatherless children due to divorce. The mocking of other children because of his eye helped him to understand the ones whose bodies were less than perfect. Being poor helped him to understand that wealth comes from me and I have given to him freely. I used every seed that started out bad and turned it into a harvest for his faithfulness. Most of all I used your lips to encourage him to serve*

*me. Every time you prayed with him I showed him my glory. He learned to run to me in the beginning. As I nurtured him he learned to walk with me. I have shown him where I brought him. My hands easily did what looked impossible to the world. I sent him to law school with a new wife and no money. I poured my spirit upon him to learn the law because he would use that to glorify me and set many of my children free. I stirred up a desire in his heart to cherish the law and I wrote it on the portals of his heart. I would take the laws he learned and nourish them with my perfect law to love others above all things. I placed him with criminal clients so that I could counsel them and change their lives."*

*"He married and longed for a son. Instead I gave him Sarah who would be a shining jewel in his crown. Differences caused him to divorce but he never let go of Sarah. He was determined to be the father he had lost when he was young. He never stopped longing for a son until one day I told him the son he wanted was in heaven with me waiting for him to come someday. At that moment he understood how great my forgiveness extends to those called by my name. He remarried someone who had a son and became a father to him. He would learn to teach this son my ways and be an example of my love. Only later in his life would he realize how important his presence was in his family's life."*

*"Every time you talked to him about me it seemed he paid no attention. I want you to know the words I spoke through your lips were seeds I planted in his heart. I watered those seeds with your prayers throughout the years. Each time a harvest was needed to glorify me the seed that was needed was used. I hope my children will grasp the importance of prayer. If a prayer is in my will it will always be answered at just the right time. Faith in Me nourishes each seed and it is faith that moves me to answer. Each day that you pray and weep over your son I take your tears and faith and water the wellspring in his life. You know I have shared his life with you. I assigned you as his spiritual guardian angel and prayed through your lips. His needs were important to me and I used you to loose my power in his life. I sent him poems and letters of encouragement*

*through your hands. I spoke to him in many ways and he learned to hear my voice."*

*"As the time drew near for him to begin counseling my people I encouraged him to be strong through the words I placed in your mouth. He heard me but was weak and needed my strength. Many trials in his life came that were used to make him strong. I allowed those trials so that he would come closer and listen to my instructions. I had you pray for him to see the world through my eyes. He began as a newborn baby. Everything was blurry in the beginning and it was hard to focus on the good. It took a lot of prayer and seeking my face to find the tiny seeds of good that were surrounded by bad in the world. I had to train him to see first what was good so that he could let me use the good seed to destroy the bad. I was preparing him to be the judge of my people and not the average judge that doesn't care. As he began to see through my eyes a burning desire started growing in his heart to reach out to my children. I saw that tiny flicker of desire begin and I flamed it with my spirit. Others around him saw the sudden change in his ways and wondered what was happening. I had changed his life and he was not aware of it in the beginning."*

*"Satan saw the work I was doing in Justin's life and began the great battle against him. He used everyone he could to try and stop my power in his life. He was called names and mocked by those who had no clue about his training. Others used his kindness and borrowed money from him for their own selfish gain. Many blamed him for their problems and stole from him. They talked behind his back and accused him of being on drugs and being gay. Lies flew everywhere but they fell on the ground and died. My warring angels destroyed all of the arrows used by Satan to destroy the destiny of my chosen one. The battle in the spiritual world was so great there soon became thousands of angels fighting the evil forces assigned against my son. He was on the training field and would come forth with a great victory. So many times you became weak from praying but I always refilled your cup of faith to overflowing to stand in Justin's behalf. Peace in his life by overcoming the great*

*battle was in sight but he must take the cloak of humility and wear it from now on."*

Mercy knew her son had worn the cloak at different times but he took it off when the world looked inviting. He had become frustrated when he wore it because there were certain ones that took advantage of him. Instead of listening to the great Counselor's voice he would give to anyone that asked and then become resentful. The takers lined up and soon he was in a hole looking up at the ones who sought to steal his blessings. She could hear him begging the Father to make them stop taking from him but she never heard him ask how to stop the madness. He was placed on her priority list of prayer. Obedience and submission must stand strong within him to overcome the bondage he had allowed to creep into his life.

*"I heard your requests for our son. I will not let go of him through this battle. Satan always brings new money into his life when he is seeking me and he starts chasing the rainbow again. You must continually pray for him to submit to me at all times. The cloak is lying by his side even now and he must put it on to hear my voice. Only until my children understand that they can do nothing without my help are they able to grow in my ways. When you pray for him I will set my angels at charge to show him they way to follow me. If you will pray with all of your heart I will hear and answer you quicker than you think. Pray for him to wear my cloak and never take it off again. The prayer requests you have asked for your own life have already been received by Me and when you pray for your soon I will pour them out into your life more than you can imagine."*

Mercy began praying for her son and as she was praying she saw so many burdens upon his back that he was bent over. She heard him groaning and gasping for breath. No wonder her Daddy had told her to pray for him. She didn't know what to pray for because they were everywhere. Some were even lying down beside him ready to attach to his back. Compassion overcame her as she raised her hands to beseech the Father on her son's behalf. The only words she could whisper were "please have mercy" as she cried in desperation. Then she began pleading the blood of Jesus on Justin. She continued to pray and she saw each burden leave her son. As they fell from him she heard him whisper "thank you" to the Father. An angel held a cup by Justin and as the tears flowed they were caught in the cup. Mercy knew her Daddy would use each tear to make beauty marks in her son's life. When each burden came forth she saw the blood of Jesus cover it and it would vanish as if it had never been there. Underneath the mass of burdens the cloak of humility began to appear. She knew she must continue to pray so every burden could be lifted from him. The power of His presence was so strong she couldn't move. Her body was trembling so hard she fell prostrate on the floor and continued to pray. There were so many angels surrounding her son she could no longer see him. She knew they were fighting a battle against Satan so she continued to pray. There were no words to describe the spiritual battle that took place. Little black deformed looking objects ran from each burden as it vanished. They were screaming and running into each other. She saw the Father stretch out His right hand and instantly they were gone. As the last burden vanished His peace began to permeate the place. The peace became so strong Mercy could only lift her head to see what was happening. She saw the angels dancing and singing around Justin. They were singing praises to God and their faces glowed so brightly she could not see them clearly. Justin slowly picked up the cloak and placed it on his shoulders. At the moment he put it on everything stood still. It was if time had stopped and the world had been put on pause.

*"I have set you free from the burdens of your past my son. I placed my calling on your life before you were even born to counsel my hurting children. There are many who counsel but there are so few that are righteous counselors. You will not be able to touch my people unless you keep the cloak on and obey my voice. The cloak carries the anointing and your obedience allows you to see the world through my eyes. I chose you to reach my children because I gave*

*you a special heart of compassion. The seed of faith you have now will grow greater than you can imagine as I do my work through you. You were given intelligence in the beginning but now I will add understanding to you. Each person I bring to you for counseling will be transparent to you. My words of healing will flow through your lips and you will see miracles before your very eyes. It will become your heart's desire to see others shed their burdens the same way you have shed yours today. As the blood of My Son transforms their lives before you each one will become your brother or sister in Christ and you will rejoice with me. I am drawing you closer to me and you will begin experiencing my glory far beyond what you could ever imagine. You will learn to clutch the cloak to you tightly and cherish its value. Satan will always be watching you and hoping you will take the cloak off. He will assign his stronger angels to destroy my work that I will perform through you. You must never forget to wear the cloak that carries my protection. I have assigned legions of my warring angels to guard you and to fight in my behalf. They will never leave your side as long as you wear the cloak. Each morning the moment you awake run to me for counsel. You will receive my instructions for that day. I will equip you with everything you will need. Never forget to come to me before you start your day lest you go out into the world without my presence upon you. I will give you a fresh, new anointing of faith each day that will be your strength and nourishment. The assignment I have given to you is greater than you can understand at this time. When you begin walking with me each day you will begin to recognize how almighty I really am. Each victory in your life will bind your heart to mine until our hearts will become as one. Very few of my children have ever experienced the relationship with me that I am offering to you now. You will represent my justice to the world. It will be their choice to accept it or refuse it. Rise up now and let us begin our work together."*

As Justin stood up the angels surrounded him with their eyes on the Father. The anointing of His presence was so strong everything stood still and was silent. Justin's face glowed from being in the Father's presence and his footsteps began to bounce as he began walking down the path of life. Everywhere he went the anointing was so strong others could feel the Father's presence. The position his Father had set aside for him to be a righteous counselor was in sight and his training was almost completed. She knew she must spend time daily and pray for her son's strength. Neither she nor her son would ever be able to describe the transformation that had taken place that day. Only the ones that became hungry enough to experience His glory would be filled with His wonders.

Mercy saw his wife Michelle standing by her son and knew she had been chosen to help him. Her character was rare and unique for she was a person of integrity who would be the stability he had always needed. She knew Michelle was the one Justin had needed to stabilize him and it was so great to know that he had found her. She saw her tender heart that had been bruised many times by others and knew that God had healing in His hands for this dear child.

*"She knows me and has my character. Integrity only comes from me and she is his example of my integrity. Manipulation has never penetrated her heart and she is honest and pure in her heart. I will show Justin to treat her as the most fragile flower that must be nurtured with love and respect at all times. She is a priceless treasure I have given to him and he must learn to treat her, as he is to treat me for I live in her. The accusing spirit he has allowed to speak through him must be removed and replaced with a spirit of trust and honor. When this happens the insecurity that attacks her will disappear and she will be covered with my peace that no one will ever take from her again. I have heard the cries of her heart and I will answer and give her rest."*

As Mercy listened to the Father speak she saw Michelle's son Collin standing close to his mother. She stood in awe as she saw the same character in him that was in Michelle. He was a boy of honor that would be respected by others because of his pureness of his heart. Humility to God would come easy for him because he knew the meaning of respect.

*"The teenage years are hard and I will touch Justin and remind him of the years of his youth when he knew me but chased the wings of excitement. I will show him how to guide and counsel his son and teach him my ways. A father is the example for a son and I will fill him with patience and understanding of the temptations of youth. As a righteous counselor he must first counsel his children so they will prosper and grow in my ways. I have drawn their hearts close to each other and Collin will listen to him. I have promised that all of your household would be saved and you will see it happen and know that my word is true."*

Mercy listened closely and she could hear her Daddy talking to Justin at that very moment. She heard Him say,

*"You will know me now as the Great Counselor. I have called you as my assistant and you will counsel my people. When you become weary with the sin that is all around you come to me and I will counsel you. You will not just represent my people but you will counsel them my way. You must tell them about me and teach them my ways. I can assure you that many will appear to reject what you say but do not be discouraged. You will plant a seed in their hearts and I will nurture that seed until it produces the result I desire. For I know the ones that will serve me and you do not. Even if some of the seeds you plant in others lives wither and die others will also be the seeds that flourish to life. Let me be the one to decide whom to send to you and you just counsel as I direct you. For have I not given you a sound mind and a tender heart? Do you not long to see my greatness in the midst of an evil world? Do not my children deserve as many chances as I have given you? Consider it a great privilege to serve me as my helper. Few look to me as a counselor. They only look to man and you are the man I am appointing to speak to those that don't know my voice. I will anoint you with a new boldness that will cause you to speak out as you have never spoken before. You will be amazed at the words that come from your mouth to defend my children. Every time you think it is not worth it just remember that I thought it was worth it to choose you to teach others. I chose Moses and he argued with*

*me saying he could not speak. In fact, Moses used every excuse he could think of because he knew in his heart that he was not worthy to be used by me. I will use you as great as I used Moses and the blood of my son that no one can accuse of sin will cover you. They may start to accuse you but no words will come forth because the blood marked you not guilty. Trust in me and see my greatness abound more than you could ever imagine."*

Then Mercy heard Justin reply,

"Oh great Counselor, how fragile is man in body and mind. I cannot grasp the greatness of your power. You are right. I would argue with you that I can only speak in the courtroom but I now understand that when I speak there it is your words. I will trust you to put the words in my mouth as I counsel your children. Help me to see deep within their hearts and not focus on their outward appearance. I have always looked at their action and never searched deeper. I boldly ask you for wisdom to serve you."

*"If you ask for wisdom you must believe that you receive it from me. It will begin as a trickle for you to grasp. As you see my profound wisdom it will grow into a mighty gushing river so great it will cause you to walk in humbleness and never look back. I will also grant you profound knowledge but you must always cherish it and never become prideful. It is so easy for man to think he knows everything when my knowledge is released. You must never forget that you knew nothing before I gave it to you. Few will understand but you will never have the words to explain to them lest pride creeps in. I am giving you a great commission and I will send you forth with my covering. As I gave instructions to my other followers so will I instruct you as we travel this road of life together."*

*"First, you must choose your staff that will up gird you and support you. This will be the first hardest task you have ever faced. You must trust me to put the right words in your mouth and obey me. Without the covering of your staff you can never serve me with power. You must let go of friendships, old debts, and old habits.*

*They are a hindrance and will cause you to stumble every day. I will not bring the right employees to you until you get rid of the old ones. Do not fear when it is just you and I that first day. For by the end of the day you will see my glory. I will bring anointed ones to support you and respect you. The ones you now have do not respect you and cause you much pain. They do not care if you do anything right and have their hand out to take what I give you. They must go. I have already placed in your heart to know what I am saying is true."*

"You are right, Mighty Counselor. I don't know how to let them go. Please show me how to do this the right way. They have been with me from the beginning and I depend on them because it is more comfortable to lean on them. I know they are not loyal and supportive, but I don't know how to find someone that will be right. They will tell others all of the wrongs of my past and ruin my name. Only you can stop this from happening. Please reassure me that you will protect me from their revenge. Now I know how Moses felt when you call him. I will trust you to handle this transition but please give me the strength to carry this through."

*"Son, when you open your mouth I will put the right words in your mouth to speak. It will be done with strength mixed with compassion. They will see you as a great leader and will leave with respect for you. In fact, the respect they never had will begin the minute you step forward in obedience to my calling. As far as others believing what they say, remember whom they will tell and that should assure you that it would not matter. I will place you in more powerful places than where you are now. You will look back and remark at your small beginnings that have been turned into powerful strides. Everything I require of you requires that you trust me and have faith in who I am. I will show myself to you and walk with you that you might know my greatness. Every time you want to look back remember all of the promises I have made to you. I will never break a promise but I bring them forth as you can handle them. You love excitement and speed so trust me whole heartedly and you will certainly see my glory all around you."*

"Great Counselor, I believe all that you say. It is easy for you to give me instructions but I am so weak when it comes to confronting others. How do I step out and do this?"

*"Do not fear what lies ahead. If I ask you to do something then I have already given you the strength to accomplish what I have asked. Keep my promises written on the rooms of your heart. You cannot put new wine into old wineskins. The wine will not be fit to drink and will rot the skins. If you do not remove all of the past including the ones that work for you then you will never succeed in my plan for you. They will hold you down and cause you to fall at every turn. Think back and remember how many times they missed a court date for you. Did I not always step in and repair the damage? Should I continue to do so after I have warned you of the consequences? I never ask you to let go of something unless I have something better for you. I have plans to prosper you and bless you as much as you can contain. I cannot bless something where there is sin in the midst. They will never change unless you initiate the change. Everyone is a creature of habit and it is I that forces the change to bring you forward into my presence. Greed and laziness have no place in my plan for your life so you must rid yourself of the ones that carry this label. Do you want the approval of sin or my approval of integrity? Integrity will never abide with greed, laziness, and a hard heart. There are some hearts that never come to life. You have done your part to make a difference so do not worry about the changes that I require you to make. Sit still as my power flows through you and I will grant you the knowing that you can step out in confidence without fear."*

"You are always right Great Counselor. You know my heart. I have contemplated taking this action for a long time now. It just never seemed the right time and guilt always surrounded me. I know that I must step forward and let you take control. Would you please give them work and keep resentment and jealousy far from their heart? You have shown me their hearts and I know only you can give me respect from their mouth. It's not just the respect. I know that I need healing from the insults they inflicted upon me in the past. Even though they never cared about my needs I still want to take care of them. Would you please help them as they go to a new way of life?"

*"Son, you are feeling my heart as you speak. I will help them as much as they will let me. What you are trying to say is that you don't want them to be mad at you. Sin is always mad when confronted by my holiness. Do you really want to be friends with sin? Yes, the male will always love you as his friend but the female will have to overcome issues in her life at first. She will hate you at first because she will feel rejected. Do not worry because she will find a new person to cling to and you will be released. Be glad and rejoice at the release of your captivity. Only when you are released will you be able to understand the strong captivity from these two that you were in for years. It began subtle and grew beyond control. I want to release this bondage as soon as possible. Can you not feel the gentle breeze of freedom beginning even as I speak? That breeze will surround you and cause you to run and leap with joy knowing there is no longer this bondage on your life. Take My hand and we will start our mission together."*

Mercy knew that God would direct her son and lead him to his calling in life. What a privilege to hear her Daddy counsel her son. She knew she must pray daily for his strength to be obedient to God and not to man.

# The Oldest Daughter

She looked down at the beautiful little girl that she had just delivered. Her beauty was breathtaking. She held the child close and asked her Father to bless her. Little did she know at the time that the blessings had already been ordered for her daughter's life. He had granted this child not only physical beauty but also a spiritual beauty that would touch millions of lives. She would carry the beauty of Christ upon her and show it to the world. It was a perfect combination perfected by the Father's hands. The potter's hands would be shaping and molding this child throughout her life to be used for His glory.

The tiny girl was named Kimberley. From the beginning she had a peaceful spirit that touched everyone around her. Her dad was crazy about her and spent time with her at every chance. She trusted him and cherished every moment they had together. She loved her mother deeply but the love of her dad was something special.

When Kim was eight years old her dad left home and never returned. Her heart was broken and she longed to spend time with him. He didn't come home for Christmas that year either. As she opened the jewelry box he had sent in the mail to her she realized this was all she had left of him. She closed that door to her heart and it would take years to visit the room in her heart that he had occupied. The battle scar on her heart would grow until many years later the Father would enter that room.

When her youngest brother, Casey was born Kim transferred her love from her dad to Casey. She carried him everywhere and told him everything she knew. She knew he would never leave her so she felt safe and secure with him. She had many friends but she never let them enter the place in her heart that had been abandoned by her dad. Only Casey was allowed in that room and they never stayed there very long.

*"I brought Curtis into her life before she was sixteen because the loneliness became too much for her to bear. You never spent enough time with her and she needed someone close. I brought Curtis because he was a faithful one and that is what she needed. His love and faithfulness was an extension of me and it gave her strength. His love was not a father's love and she kept searching. She found another that became the father of her daughter but I took him because he was not the one chosen for her life. Curtis knew me and his love for her was never ending even when she walked away. He cried out for me to bring her back but she did not listen. I took the tears he cried and healed his broken heart. Although they were apart the bond of love they had, as friends would never be destroyed. Binding hearts together is one of the things I enjoy doing the most. When I am in the midst of that bond it becomes so strong the cord cannot be broken. That is the power of my love."*

*"The guilt of leaving Curtis haunted Kim as she searched for something she was not sure of. She met someone who thought she was physically beautiful and she thrived thinking this was the answer. She endured abuse to punish herself for the mistakes she had made and the pain she had caused others. It was at this time I drew that broken heart to me and began to heal her. No one but Kim and I know the pain she endured before I rescued her. Her heart laid at my feet shattered into a million pieces. Each tear*

*she cried I placed in my cup as I held her close. Together we began to pick up each piece of her heart. We washed each piece with a tear she had cried and held it together with my engulfing love. Her battle for love would be the greatest beauty mark she would ever receive. I filled her with so much of my love that neither one of us could move for the longest. She had come home to me and the angels began rejoicing. I handed her the cloak of humility and she covered herself completely. She tried to look back at Curtis but I encouraged her to love him and let him live in peace at this time. She agreed and I began carrying her until she was strong enough to walk. Her destiny was in sight and I had great plans for her."*

The tears would not stop flowing from Mercy's face as she sat at her Daddy's feet. She asked him to heal her daughter's heart from the hurts she had unknowingly caused in her life. The pain was tremendous as she realized she had never been there when Kim needed her. She asked the Father for forgiveness and he wiped the tears from her eyes and caught them in the cup. She wondered how she could ever mend the relationship she had not nourished during all of those years when it had been so important. Only the Father could repair the damage she had caused and breathe life into a new relationship with her daughter.

*"I know what you are feeling and I want to reassure you that I have taken care of the damage. I have already started binding your hearts together and you will be closer in hearts and spirits than you could dream was possible. I will do this great work between you and Kim now so that you both can be healed completely. The need she had for you will be filled and I will erase the memories that brought her pain during those trying times. I have great things in store for her life and you will be her prayer warrior every day without fail. Write her letters of encouragement often and call her and tell her you love her. Your love combined with my great love will nourish her every day. Do not fear. She has tasted my love and will not look back to the artificial love the world has to offer. She will share it with others and my anointing will touch their hearts.*

*Her heart and spirit will be more beautiful than her physical body. She will be the jewel in your crown that shines the brightest."*

Mercy was overcome with emotion as her Daddy held her daughter. He told her Kim was the one to take his love to this hurting world. The power of His presence upon her life would cause demons to flee in fear and all that would be left around her would be His love. Others would feel His presence and be healed in many ways. He would write movies through her hands and speak through her mouth everywhere she went. His great compassion would flow from her heart and she would console the unlovely in spirit. His angels would never leave her side and she would walk in peace being led by His spirit. The calling on her daughter's life was so great Mercy was in awe. The Father had taken a child forsaken and filled her with His love. His great love would be used to change the hearts of many of His children through Kim. What an honor to be chosen as the mother of someone that would be used so greatly by the King. It was so amazing that He could take all the mistakes that Mercy had made and turn them into miracles.

God not only healed Kim's heart but He brought Kent into her life. At that very time he was going through a divorce and needed someone to care. Kim cared for him and began teaching him my ways. Their love for each other grew and I bound their hearts together.

*"I have great plans for Kim and Kent's lives. As they draw closer to me I will place my anointing upon them to touch others in a way no one else can do. I will use Kent's hands to make the unlovely in body beautiful again. Those that need my help will touch his heart and I will heal them with his hands. He has a great calling upon his life to serve me. I have healed him of his past and it will never return. The healing has given him the freedom to serve me as he has been called to serve. As he begins to touch others he will be overcome with compassion for them and my love will flow through him to touch their hearts. Together Kent and Kim will move throughout the world touching others lives. Many times they will not even realize all of the ones I have touched through them*

*but their kindness and caring will penetrate even the hardest of hearts. Kent's sons, Blake and Will already seen the change in their dad's life and will follow in his footsteps as they grow older. Blake already has my heart and knows me. I will do a special healing in Will's heart and the abandonment he has felt will be replaced with a new peace. He will grow to love his family and finally feel secure with them. Until now he has been afraid the new family would disappear just like his other family did. I will teach Kent to counsel him in my ways and how to understand his heart. Kim will nurture him with love and he will begin to seek me. When he seeks me he will find me and his heart will be healed and set free."*

Mercy thought back and remembered how heavy Kim was on her heart on Mother's Day a few years ago. She wanted to tell her so many things but didn't know where to begin. After much thought, she wrote this letter to her.

*A* Mother's Words

I thought it would be nice to give you the best gift I could offer on Mother's day so here goes written just for you.

When you were born the minute I saw you I knew you had a great destiny. You were chosen for such a time as this to make a difference.

I remember your smiles, your laugh, and your sweetness through all of the years. I don't remember problems or differences but only the tender moments when we were the closest and shared our deepest secrets. I hurt when you hurt, cried when you cried, and even cried when I thought you hurt but never told me. It is so rare that we take the time to tell others just how much they mean to us and that is why I am writing this to let you know how much I love you.

You are the most considerate and caring of all of my children. God sees all of everything in your life and tells me how to pray for you. If you will stay humble to God and strong against the world you will walk in peace and God will guide your footsteps. I have learned to walk in peace no matter what I confront because I spend time in prayer each day and it is more effective if you do it early in the morning. That will give you wisdom and the power of the Holy Spirit to conquer anything that happens during the day. Then you will always walk in peace. When you walk in peace you will walk in blessings because you will be walking in faith. Only faith moves mountains and causes God to do the impossible, so if something looks impossible to you rejoice because that means God will do the thing you could never do to begin with.

If you begin waking early in the mornings just know that I am already awake praying for your wisdom and peace for the day. God takes each battle scar in life and makes it a beauty mark because unless there is a battle there is no victory. If you will keep your eyes on Him He will win every battle you will ever face. Now is the time for you to step out and fulfill your heart's desire. God gave you that desire which means He will fulfill it if you just trust Him. You have such a great anointing of Godly wisdom that I know you will have favor when you step out in faith. Just ask God to open the doors where He wants you to go and close the ones where you don't belong.

I hope these words will make a difference in your life. Just remember no one told me these things and I had to learn them from experience. Never forget my great love for you because that love will give you the strength to reach higher than you can see because you know I believe in you. Even when I don't get to see you or even talk to you just know you are always in my heart and on my mind.

I love you,

Mom

Mercy suddenly realized that after she wrote this letter to Kim their hearts became bound together as one. They became close and shared their deepest feelings with each other. God had taken the words He had given Mercy to write to her daughter and healed both of their hearts of their painful past. She began to understand just how powerful His words were and they breathed life into the ones that He sent them to hear. Her daughter had such a compassion for others and Mercy knew she would touch many lives with her great caring spirit.

One day Kim called and said she felt a great calling to minister to hurting men. When she and Kent went to visit at a prison she saw a black man sitting with his girlfriend during the visitation time. She saw deep within him helplessness where he had given up hope to ever survive. God whispered to her to go and minister to him. She told him that God loved him and to never give up hope because God cared for him and was going to do something great in his life. A tiny spark of hope flickered in his eyes and Kim began to pray for him daily. She had planted the seed of hope on barren ground but only God could water it and cause it to grow. Mercy and Kim agreed that they both would pray for him each day and would believe that God would never let that seed of hope die. They would believe that God would water it with His spirit and bring him back to the fullness of life that God had intended for him to have. Mercy realized that most of the time we plant one seed at a time but that one seed will be multiplied many times over from one person to another. Some children are called to plant seeds and others are called to water the seeds that have been planted. God will take the seed and bring it to maturity with His great love and mercy.

*"I have bound the hearts of Kent and Kim together as one. They will take my love to the hurting and outcast. Did I not take them to Peru to see the poverty and sickness of my children there? This was their first mission for me and their hearts will never be the same. Kent did surgery on children with deformities that would have never had the chance to be touched by me. His heart went out to them and he felt compassion on the doctor who was so underpaid but kept working to help his people. I will use Kent's hands and Kim's heart to make a difference in many lives. They will work together to*

*touch others that are hard to reach and the ones that are forgotten by the world. The pain of their past will be turned into joy as they see my glory. How I long to use all of my children and pour out my love on a hurting world but most of the world has a cold heart that seeks worldly riches instead of heavenly riches. Because of their abundance of compassion for my children spiritual blessings and material riches will be added unto them because I can trust them. The eyes of their understanding have been opened and no longer do they look at what they have in the world but what they have with me."*

Mercy thought of the many times she had gone and worked for them when they went on trips. Every person that called their office said they were so loving and kind. What a compliment for her children. Although the world did not always recognize it they saw the love of God pouring out from them to others.

Every time Mercy went to their house she was filled with peace while she was there. It always felt like being on the mountaintop in the midst of God's presence. She could hardly wait to get there because He always came and touched her in a special way. His presence was so refreshing she always hated to leave. It was just she and her Master and every thing in the world was forgotten except His presence.

# The Youngest Son

He wasn't planned and came unexpected. His dad had just left home when Mercy found out about him. She began praying over his life not knowing what would be in store for him with no earthly father. Every night while she was carrying him before he was born she would play Christian music and sing softly to the tiny one she would bare. A knowing surrounded her that this child would be used greatly by the Father. She asked her Daddy to be the father to him during his entire life. Mercy's prayer was received and answered even before the child was born.

His name was Casey and he was surrounded by the love of his family. He never seemed to suffer the loss of the presence of his dad. Instead, he worked hard in school and Mercy quickly saw that he had been given a mind that only the Father could create. She began praying every morning for wisdom with her son and he excelled in school. He was easy going and had the gentlest spirit she had ever seen in a child. There was not a lot of money but there was always an abundance of love.

*"I claimed him while he was young. We spent time together every day and he told me everything in his heart. When you would ask for wisdom for him he always believed he had it and I gave it to*

*him freely. You never knew many of the pains he had during the growing years. Rejoice that he brought them all to me because he knew I would help him. My anointing has always been strong on his life even though many times he has run from me. Every time he ran away he would run back into my arms because He knew I would never leave his side."*

*"Our son ran away from me when he was in college. Satan used alcohol to find acceptance in a world he was not used to being in. Even though he ran away he would come and visit me when there were problems and I chased Him for many years. He learned the power of my presence and always came back. He met the preppie world while at Harvard Law School but they were never able to steal his heart away. Satan used a woman there to tempt him into their world but I held him back. I had placed a calling on his life and removed anyone and anything that might prevent him from serving me. He knows what I am talking about and I am telling you this to let you know that I never let go of him. Every time you prayed the angels surrounded him and sent the demons flying that were trying to lure him into their world. You always prayed for his safety and wisdom and I honored every prayer. The details are for Casey and I alone to review and settle between us. Pray for him every morning and my angels will go before him no matter where I send him. Some day soon he will realize you are his prayer warrior and then he will understand why I chose you for his mother."*

Mercy was overwhelmed at the awesomeness of her Daddy. She had always complained that He took so long to answer her prayers. She was just now realizing He answers the prayers in His will before they ever leave her mouth. Just because she did not immediately see the answers did not mean He had not moved His mighty right hand of power. Sometimes He even gave blessings when they were not requested. All of her children were not a blessing she had not asked for nor had she planned. She had thought all of this time that her purpose in life was somewhere in the future when all of the time it was to raise extraordinary children for His kingdom. He had even removed their earthly fathers so he could teach them. It was so true that His ways are perfect and above her understanding.

*"I placed a hunger in Casey's heart to learn the law. He is finding that the laws that were set in place many years ago are no longer there to protect the innocent but to protect the wealthy. The laws of the world are no longer in line with my laws and have become so complex their interpretation can be twisted to fit a situation. I will place him in training under one of my chosen ones in a most unusual way. I will position him in high places to make the changes that must take place. He must first take off the old self of worldliness and begin wearing my cloak of humility. I have allowed him to run free for a time to learn the ways of the world. Soon there will come the time that he must begin training for my kingdom. You must pray for him each morning that he will hear my voice and be obedient to my calling. There are many plans that I have that are too wonderful to explain at this time."*

Mercy knew her son was in training and the training was hard. She spent a lot of time in prayer for God to touch him and protect him. One day when she was in prayer she saw Casey running as fast as he could run. She didn't see anything or anyone else so she asked God whom he was running from.

*"He is running from me but he doesn't know it. He is afraid to let go and let me have control of his life. He thinks he must prove to the world that he is successful. If he would stop long enough to listen to me I would tell him that I am the only success that there is in the world. I have let him run for some time now and soon he will be tired and want to rest. In his weariness he will remember in the days past how beautiful my presence was in his life. Then he will call out to me and I will answer him and show him great and mighty things he never knew."*

*"Until now he has not had to face major battles in his life but soon he will realize I am the only one to win the battle he is now facing.*

*I will bring to his memory the many words you have spoken to him during the past and he will begin to seek me for answers."*

*"Do not be concerned about what is taking place in his life now because I will never leave him unprotected and no harm will come to him. He will think his life is in ruins but you will know that it is being put back together with my hands. When I put his life back together he will be filled with my strength and courage. He has always been filled with my wisdom but when I renew his mind he will have a double portion of wisdom that he has never known before. This time it will be Godly wisdom adorned with my favor to be taken to high places that few people ever see. He must first put on the cloak of humility so that I can shine through him and keep him from falling. I will remove all of the old habits, friends, and wrong thinking that have caused him not to grow in my ways."*

*"I promise you as his mother that I will never leave him and I will protect him from all harm. He knows the power of my presence. He will soon hunger for my presence and start spending time with me. I heard your request to draw him close to you and share his life with you and he will do this soon. He will begin to see the anointing of my spirit upon your life and trust you, as he never has before. My hand will break the shell he has tried to build around his heart gently and I will release the tender heart that has been in bondage for years. He will begin to see through my eyes and feel with my heart. It will be so breathtaking to him he will never go back to where he came from. I will do this work quickly in his life and set him free. He has been hurting and searching too long and it is time for all bondages to fall from his life."*

Mercy had been praying for Casey for so long she could hardly wait for God to catch him and set him free. He had run so long she knew he was weary and ready for the peace only God can give to him. She saw the pride leave him and an aura of integrity took its place. God had chased her son and caught him. Now he would learn to chase God and taste His goodness and want more of Him each day.

*"Casey is the loyal child I gave you. His heart has always been pure and he believes in truth and justice. He has my caring heart and is always there for anyone. Every friend he ever made has always stayed friends with him because of his loyalty. He has wanted to be independent so badly that he has never reached out to anyone in his time of need. He has always been my son and I have cared for him even when he did not ask me to care. His burdens have become heavy and he is now reaching out to me because he knows my presence. When he comes before me he always wears the cloak of humility and gives reverence to me. He has faced many trials recently and I have filled him with wisdom. Pray for him to have courage to step out and follow my instructions. I am leading him to a place where he will have to have the courage that David had to handle his decisions."*

# The Youngest Daughter

The last child was neither planned nor expected. No one knew but Mercy that she would arrive until the day she was born. Kim wanted to run away and Casey cried. Justin was excited and was the only one to visit her in the hospital. She was named Ashley and was so tiny she wore doll clothes for the first month. God had plans for her that was bigger than anyone would imagine at the time. Her dad brought his new girlfriend to see her when she came home. He told Mercy she was ugly and laughed at her. Mercy cried and wondered why no one understood her situation.

*"No one knew the purpose of this child in your life. She would be your strength many times and you would be her mentor. She was physically beautiful but I gave her a special heart to love the unlovely. So few of my children can love without reserve and see goodness in everything but I gave this special talent to Ashley. She has always seen the world through my eyes and looked for the good instead of trying to pinpoint the bad in others. She was chosen to carry the torch of my love to everyone she comes in contact with. My touch through her will change many lives and she will serve me with obedience. You didn't know it but when I gave her a daughter she began to wear the cloak of humility. I placed a special anointing on her that will never be removed. Be careful to always uplift her*

*because she looks to you for guidance. You leaned on her during the hard years and she struggled to take care of you. I allowed this for her to become strong in spirit. Do not lean on her any longer but encourage her to lean on you when she is weak. Then I will speak through your lips the encouragement she needs to serve me. When she becomes strong enough I will lift her up to a higher level in her service to me. I chose you to be a special prayer warrior as she grows in my care. Trust me to use her obedience to me in a way that will be amazing. Her heart has become like pure gold and is priceless in my eyes."*

Mercy looked and she saw the angels surrounding her daughter. There were so many and they were all looking toward heaven with their hands raised high in praise to the Father. They had formed a circle of protection around her she saw the demons running away in every direction. The anointing encased her and her face was radiant from His presence. She knew He was sending her forth to touch the hearts of His children. She would be a counselor to the hearts of a hurting generation. It was a special calling upon her life. She would be used to reach the ones that no one else could reach. A special compassion for the poor, homeless, and fatherless children who had suffered much and lost hope would consume her and flow through her being.

*"Her daughter Trinity was given as a special gift to her in her youth. Trin will be an extension of Ashley's calling and will carry the torch for her when she is grown. Even now Trin listens to my voice and has my mind. I have already begun to prepare her for my service. She has been given a special understanding and discernment of the spiritual world. She has a fighting spirit that will cause the demons to flee when they come near her. I have given her a special strength to win battles that others have surrendered in. She carries your presence in her heart at all times and talks to you when she needs you with her. I have given you a special hearing to hear her when she calls you even though she has no phone. You will have spiritual ears from this day on to know her voice regardless of any other noise around you. Answer her and she will listen to you.*

*There will be many who will mock you and say this is not possible but I have already told you that what is impossible with man is always possible with Me. Always be careful to represent my purity to her so that she will be a shining example to others. Trinity will be used greatly to unite hearts and lives of those whose hearts have hardened. Encourage her continually to trust me and be an example of my character. Time is of urgency and I have begun my work in Ashley at a very young age. I will use her to reach my people while there is still time."*

Mercy knew her Daddy had spoken and she gave thanks to Him for choosing her family to touch a hurting world. She looked and saw the tiniest mantle draped across her granddaughter's heart. Trinity's blue eyes were glistening and she danced with excitement. Although her clothes were not name brand ones she was wearing a cloak designed by the Master's hands. She also knew that this child would face many trials in life because of the choices she had made. She had been so strong and cared for Trin through all of her young years and become strong in handling responsibility. Ash was the sweetest of all of the children and at the same time the weakest in handling problems. Mercy knew that God would be working on her emotions to help her be strong and still be caring. That was a balance so few learned in life but it would be a challenge that Ash would overcome.

Mercy looked and saw Ash overcoming all of the obstacles that Satan tried to place on her path. She wanted to make a difference and she was doing just that. She began counseling her friends and praying for her own family out of her desperate need for her own help in coping with her life. The more she counseled and cared for others the greater God's love poured from Ash's heart which was healing for the pain of her past.

*"I healed her pain with my great love. Her heart was so tender I held her for many years to keep my strength flowing through her. I reminded her of all the words of encouragement you had spoken to her during the years. Now she has grown in me and knows my*

*heart. I will use her greatly to encourage and uplift others who need me. When this child prays I hear her and answer her. She knows my voice and is becoming obedient to my instructions. Her brother has always shown a difference between her and the other children and her heart has bled with hurt all of these years. He also listens to my voice and I will counsel him about the hurt he has caused her. He learned prejudices from his dad and many have been instilled in his heart for years although he would deny it. This always gave him the excuse to not help her in her time of need. I am going to remove the prejudice from him once and for all. Then he will realize just what a wonderful person this child really is."*

Mercy knew what God had spoken was true. She also knew that his wife loved Ash very much and defended her often. There was really not anyone that couldn't love and admire her. She had overcome adversity from all directions and emerged with an abundance of God's love flowing from her heart. She had no resentment or revenge near her and would be the one that kept the family bound together. This reminded Mercy of the many years she had tried to win her brother's approval to no avail. She knew how painful it was to be rejected and alone. There would be a time when her brother who she longed to please would truly accept Ash. They would become very close after he realized the shame he had done.

When Ash was a small child Mercy had named her Lulu. She was always busy talking to everyone and listening to what they said. She had suffered much during her childhood years as the other children called her fat and made fun of her. She felt inferior to her older sister who had always been small and petite. In her later years she learned that she could control her weight but she didn't do it to please others. Instead, she did it to feel good about herself.

Trin's father walked away and never returned after she was born. The loss was great to Ash. She had loved him but she knew he would never take care of her and Trin. He had never had anyone teach him loyalty or even anyone that had really loved him his entire life. There would be a day when he would want his family and it would be too late.

Ashley met Zack and they became best friends. They shared their deepest secrets and the friendship grew into a lasting love. He was a wonderful father to Trin and loved her without reserve. He was the one that taught Trin about life and they had a bond that could not be broken.

No one in his family helped him financially and he became a self made man who had learned from experience. He, too, learned to trust in God because there was no one else to help him be strong and take care of his family. Together Ash and Zack covered Trin with love and attention and she grew strong in her faith in God.

# Her Children's Children

The tiny girl was given to Kim unexpectedly. She had the voice of an angel and was beautiful to see. Curtis was appointed as her earthly father and loved her with all of his heart. This child was very special to the heavenly Father and her heart was bound to His so tightly He would never let her go. Many would be her trials in life but she would love Him with a love unceasing.

*"I gave Randi the inheritance of heaven because Satan took her inheritance on earth. She was given a special heart that did not long for the material things others her age thought about. Her voice would be used for my service and sing my praises. She felt forsaken by all in her youth but she clung to me for comfort. She has a forgiving heart that holds no grudges and she believes in those no one else has faith in. Her heart has been bruised and stomped on many times but it belongs to me and I have repaired it often during the years. When the pain became almost unbearable I gave her a daughter to hold close for comfort. The trusting heart and believing spirit in Randi was given to her daughter to be carried on throughout all of her generations to come. They have my heart and my favor will be upon them all the days of their life. No matter what devices are plotted against them by Satan I will overcome him in their life. Your love and encouragement will be used to nourish*

*them when they are weak and it will give them strength. They will know you are their prayer warrior and will run the race of life with zest."*

What a beautiful gift of love the Father had given her. He had claimed even her grandchildren for His glory. She knew He would be their provider when there was no one else to care for them. His very presence would be the power in their life to keep trying when everything seemed impossible and His angels would protect them from all harm. She saw the great granddaughter that had not yet been born holding Randi's hand. They were walking side by side and the Master was leading the way. What a comfort it was to know they were in the Master's care.

The tiny girl was a gift of love given to her parents. She was named Sarah and was gentle in spirit. Her heart was crushed before she turned two years old. For many years she kept wishing her parents would be together once more.

Her parents placed her in a private Christian school when she was three and she met the Master there. He healed her heart and taught her His ways and she learned to laugh again. Only her dad saw the trauma she had felt and realized the effect it had on her life. He poured out his love for this beautiful child and their hearts became as one. Mercy became a place of refuge for Sarah when she needed special attention and extra love. They spent time together laughing and going places. Sarah had such a beautiful spirit that Mercy was determined to encourage her to have faith in the Master.

*"She began to understand the power of my presence the time you took her to visit Ashley. On the way home it was raining so hard you couldn't see to drive and the windshield wipers did not work. Sarah was engulfed in fear and asked you to pray to me. You asked me to stop the rain until you got home. I parted the rain around you and although it was raining heavily all around it did not rain on you. Remember Sarah kept saying, "God and Jesus are the greatest"? I*

*filled her heart that night with my presence and her faith began to soar. From then on Sarah knew to pray and she knew I was with her. She carries my anointing that is rare and precious. You will never know how many times she has asked for to have her mommy and daddy live together. Someday I will use her to unite families and children. She will serve me with fierceness because she knows I care about my children. You are to pray for her each day so that Satan cannot touch her pureness in this dark world. Her gentle heart is priceless and I will nurture it with the love her family gives to her. I have given her an intelligence of this world that exceeds most of my children because she listens to my voice. Her mind is a treasure chest that I fill daily with wisdom that comes only from me. She will be the bridge between her parents that unites love to her heart. I have given her favor wherever she goes and I will guide her and protect her. Spend time with her and nurture her with your love."*

Mercy knew she must pray for Sarah fragile heart every day without fail. The cloak of humility had been extended from her dad to her and prayer would protect her from the world.

# Her Brother

She got the call unexpectedly. It was her brother and she had not heard from him in years. He was thirteen years older than her and had always been her hero. Many times she had wanted to reach out and spend time with him but he had always been too busy for her. He had seemed so successful and she had been so poor many of the years they had been apart. She had never wanted him to know of her hardships for fear he might consider her a failure.

He told Mercy he had been diagnosed with brain tumors and would be coming for treatment in Austin. Her heart broke as she heard the fear in his voice. Two years before she had prayed and asked her Daddy to reunite them back together. That prayer was being answered now as she talked to him at length.

He came to Austin and Mercy went to see him when he came. All hurts from the past had vanished and her love for him was great. She was so ashamed that she had not included him in her prayers all of these years. He was a man of integrity in all of his ways and had a sensitive heart. She was determined to be with him from then on and she told him how much she had missed him and how she loved him.

She saw him grow weaker and weaker and it soon was so bad he had to stay in an assisted living home. As she spent many hours sitting by his side she encouraged him to have faith in God. She told her Daddy that if He had to take him to please not let him be in pain.

*"I heard your prayer and honored it. Your presence with him gave him peace and overcame the fears he felt. There was a bond of forgiveness between the two of you and I covered it with my love. He saw your loyalty and knew you really cared for him. You never let yourself grieve his loss and you never let go of him when I took him to myself. Let me hold you now and catch the tears you have held back. I will use those tears to heal your heart from the past. I am your Comforter and your Healer. I specialize in broken hearts and broken dreams. Rest in Me now."*

As the words sunk in from her Daddy, Mercy laid her head down and began crying. The tears flowed for hours. He led her back over all the years of absence and the pain was so great she didn't know if she could go through the journey. Little treasures she had held so close to her surfaced and she cherished each one.

Mercy remembered the time Buddy had called when she was six years old. He was in the Navy and had called home to tell everyone he was okay. When she heard his voice on the phone she started crying and ran and hid. She missed him so much she cried all night wanting him to come home. He was her hero and she had to see him.

Buddy came home and she never left his side. One day he was ironing his white starched pants and she ran into his leg. He yelled at her to back off. Then he spanked her in his anger. Mercy was crushed and she limped into the bedroom and lay motionless on the bed. She would never make him mad at her again she vowed because he was her hero.

The most amazing thing about Buddy was that Mercy knew his heart. She saw him as a sensitive, loving person that never showed a lot of emotion. He was a perfectionist and a man of integrity. She wanted these attributes and he became her role model. She never wanted to disappoint someone with this great character. She thought everything he did was perfect and she must be the same way.

Mercy remembered when her first husband left her. She was pregnant with Casey and broken hearted. Both her dad and Buddy asked her what she did for him to leave. Their questions broke her heart and she felt worthless. From that time on she saw herself as a failure and avoided going to see the ones she loved so much.

*"You wanted to be perfect so badly that you gave up. I turned that situation into good for you. Your weakness became the place I could exalt my strength and I nourished a loving heart deep inside of you. Without that weakness you could not have worn the cloak of humility. You never knew how much love you radiated to everyone around you because it was I that shined from you. My spirit touched everyone you came into contact with and there was great resentment from those with a hard heart. They mocked you and said you tried to portray "poor little me" because they could not understand your humbleness. The seeds of love I planted into all of those hearts you came into contact with will be nourished with the tears you are crying now. Rejoice that the pain you felt will be used to glorify me. The shame you felt will be turned into great beauty marks to those years will be filled with the joy of the children I have blessed you with. I allowed all of these things in your life to make you the person you are today. I never left your side even when you tried to hide from me. I have used the curses spoken against you to become the integrity you have so desired all of your life. Not all will see the beauty of my hand in your life but even one person that grasps my greatness shining forth from your pain will be worth it all. I don't count the number of ones I touch through you. Instead, I count the faithfulness of your heart that serves me."*

She saw her brother lying on the bed wrapped in a new humbleness that she had never seen in him before. He picked up her hand and kissed it gently. Their hearts became bound together at that moment. She knew she must be there for him until the end. She sat by his side for hours and fed his drops of water through a straw. This time the bond of love could not be broken as they shared the last days together. As she massaged his body with lotion she asked her Daddy to please not let him hurt. Sometimes she would step outside and cry because of the helplessness of her brother.

One day Mercy went back into Buddy's room after crying quietly outside. As she stepped close to him she saw that cloak of humility glowing from his fragile body. It was so beautiful she couldn't move for the longest time. Their eyes met and she knew her Daddy had shown him the kingdom and he was now at peace. His presence filled the room and she felt the angels all around. That night he told her that he had seen their mother and dad and they were waiting for him in heaven. He didn't want anyone to be upset with him leaving but he had to go. She wasn't ready for him to leave. They needed to make up all the years of being apart. The only way she could face the loss was that she knew her Daddy had chosen her to lead her brother to the gates of heaven. He had a glow about him and she knew he had been close to the Father. She whispered, "I love you" at every chance and held his hand for hours. The end was near and she wanted to send him home covered in her love. The love of a few months was so great it covered all of the years of silence. She had not experienced the beauty of the cross in this magnitude before but it was breathtaking. That cloak she held so dear had covered her family. It could not be taken from them. All that was left was His presence. What a beautiful gift from her Daddy to give her the last months of Buddy's life. Never again would she let pride keep her from touching the lives of everyone around her.

*"I woke you up when I sent the angels for him. He knew you were there as he entered my gates. He is resting with me now and the family is waiting for you. I have more work for you to do yet and a*

*little more polishing on your jewels. You know I use you to polish the jewels that I gave to you. They must be prepared to release you to me. I heard your whisper for me to heal your relationship with Buddy the moment you asked me. You didn't know how to reach out to him but I did. I placed you in his dreams, his thoughts, and his heart. Everywhere he went you were there. Because of My great love he reached out to you when he needed you and I made it possible. Does this not show you how I listen to every tiny prayer you pray and care about your concerns? It is my love that heals a heart and makes all things right. I want you to smile when I brush him against your mind from now on and know that I did a special miracle for you that no one could take from you. Cherish the memories and be glad that you could share the ending of his chapter in this world. The ending is very special for my chosen ones because I shine my brightest. Rejoice for every tear. They are used to heal the broken hearted and to set the captives free from the chains that bound them on earth. My love is ever lasting and my compassion is endless for the ones who wear the cloak."*

The gentle mist of the rain was consoling as she watched it falling so quietly. She could feel it washing her very soul of the past that had held so much pain. As had been so common in the last few years the only strength she felt was His presence. The anointing was so strong she dared not move. He was here and He always brought healing in His wings. She was determined to sit as still as possible no matter how long it took for Him to speak. She knew He was standing in the shadows and His love began to envelope her from head to toe. She trembled as she felt Him draw close and fell face down to worship her Master. His spirit was gentle but so powerful she dared not look up in her humanness.

*"I have healing in my wings for you today. You will no longer remember the pain of your past. Where there was sorrow there will now be joy knowing I brought good things to replace the bad that so plagued you. This cleansing had to take place for you to be at peace with those who hurt you and tried to shame you. I have not forgotten my covenant with you and I am bringing it forth*

*now. I will breathe life on every heart's desire I have given to you. You asked for me to help you leave an inheritance for your children and it is here. The home I have given you will be used for my glory through all of your children. They will house the homeless, feed the hungry, and clothe the ones in need. Most importantly, they will teach the downcast my word and lead them to me. This is a mighty act that can only be performed from me and all will see my glory".*

*"I heard you the time you asked to be just like Jesus. It was then I began a great work in your life. You couldn't understand why you were mocked, talked about, and walked in poverty. I allowed that for your good. He suffered all of these things while on earth. You experienced His hurt and suffering. To reach the hurting ones you had to experience their suffering to understand them. It taught you to have compassion for the ones rejected by the world because of their lack. It gave you insight to look into the eyes of everyone you meet and know their pain. I came to save the unlovely and the ones rejected by the world. The more you serve me the more you will be rejected by the ones that don't know me".*

*"My word says that when you see a brother in need help him but the world is full of greed and says he brought his situation on himself. Only my unconditional love can touch the ones that are defeated. My pure love cannot be given through anyone until all unforgiveness is gone. There is a special mission I have for you that will complete your healing and set you free at last. Listen closely and I will tell you what it is now."*

She heard the whisper in her heart. It was the voice she loved more than anyone else. She knew her Daddy was preparing her for a great miracle and the anticipation was great. Who would He touch through her this time she wondered. It always seemed to be the most unexpected person who crossed her path. Somehow this time the mission seemed different as if it were a matter of life and death. It was urgent and Mercy grasped the cloak tightly to her body in reverence. If it was as great as she felt it was then she must let Him flow through her without interruption. She felt weak but excited knowing how great it is to serve the Master. She knew He would never disappoint her and if He asked her to be obedient then she must listen carefully.

*"The one I wish to touch this time is very depressed and has almost given up hope on any happiness in his life. It will take months of preparation for me to use you to touch him. There is only one way to penetrate the pride and distrust he has in his heart. I must warn you that the accuser will attack you mightily in the beginning and his goal is to make you feel defeated. He will tell you this is your idea and that you are not in my will but you know my voice. My voice will envelope your heart and shut his mouth as long as you wear the cloak. This will be the hardest mission I have ever asked of you. Before I tell you who he is you must commit to this calling. You will be so weak at times when the attacks are the strongest that I will carry you. It is in your weakness that my strength is made perfect and my will is done. Do not be afraid for I will go before you. The battle is not yours. You will be my voice and my presence in his life where there is no longer any hope. The time will come when he will see my goodness in your life and then he will have hope in me. You forgave him years ago and set him free but he does not know that yet. I will come to him through you and set him free. No matter what he says or does you must let my love and presence shine through you. The ending will be beautiful and it will be the greatest miracle you have yet to experience. The angels will be your constant protectors and they will surround you at all times. It is now that you will begin to understand how important even one child is to me. So many want to touch millions but I tell you that even one life is my goal. I will use you to release the chains of bondage and set the captive free. Now let me hold you and fill you with my strength."*

As Mercy rested in her Daddy's arms she wondered who this person was that was so important to her Master. She didn't want to ask Him who it was out of respect. He would tell her when it was time. After all of the years of impatience she was learning that His plan would be perfect. What an honor to serve the most high God and be chosen by Him. She knew she could do nothing without His help so she began spending hours in prayer before Him. When the training was hard she would fast for three days and seek Him with all of her heart. He always came and encouraged her to keep going forward in their quest.

As time went on she learned to be obedient no matter what He asked her to do. He moved Ashley to an apartment and she was completely alone. There was no more support group and someone to lean on. It would just be her Daddy and her.

The insurance agency she had dried up and there was no income. Mercy fasted for three days for help. A woman at the church told her to call Visiting Angels. It was a health agency ran by Christians and they hired her that very day. She was shocked that He would place her in health care. She knew nothing about the medical field and had not ever taken care of the elderly. It was income and she knew He had placed her there for a reason.

*"You were placed there to be a part of my preparation in bringing these children to My Kingdom. Some knew about me. Others learned about me through you. As my love flowed through you and you touched them gently with your hands they knew I was there. Every child I sent you to had my legions of angels caring for them. You developed a compassion for the ones who had been forgotten by their families and society. You were the daughter who rarely came to visit and the old friend who was too busy to care. Satan could not come near them in your presence and they experienced the peace that only I can give. I molded you in gentleness and love that filled their empty hearts. I was the voice calling to them in their desert and the touch that had been gone for years. They poured out their hearts to you and learned to trust you because of your caring heart. You bowed by their bed and prayed for them with all of your heart. This restored the dignity they felt robbed of because of their frailness. Their children rejoiced that you did the work they were appointed to do to honor their parents. I never let you stay with anyone very long lest a dependence on you would happen.*

*When they saw me in your life I removed you and took your place. I moved through you just enough to capture their heart and then I took over and released you from their care. You saw them through my eyes and loved them with my love."*

Mercy cried as her Daddy shared His greatness with her. He had sent her to millionaires who lived like hermits. Their money could not buy love nor could it restore the dignity that had been lost through the years. Only the touch of the Master could restore what Satan had stolen from their lives and fill them with His peace. In the beginning they considered her their servant and they didn't know that she was a servant of the King. She was paid less than she had ever made but the rewards from her Daddy were priceless. Everyone looked down on her and thought her work was embarrassing. They didn't know that the King had ordered this work. As she looked back she realized He had used her to break the yolk of bondage off of the children she had been sent to help. She appeared to each one as poor because she was not materially wealthy. Each one learned that she was spiritually rich and wanted what she had. She radiated the Father's presence and it melted the greed and pride from each one she had touched. Their investments and money could never buy what they lacked. She had been sent to each one to set them free from the chains they had worn for years by leaving His presence with them. She realized suddenly that the cloak had never been removed since she had been listening to her Daddy's voice.

When the call came about her brother she knew she had been trained to help him in time of need. She cared for him as if she had been a nurse most of her life. They shared their hearts and his last months became filled with peace from the Father. She prayed for him and led him to the gates of heaven knowing he was with their Father eternally. All of the criticism and misunderstanding of her mission was worth it all to serve the Master. The blessing of spending the last days with her brother was worth it all. No one in all of the wealth had given her anything material but she had received the wealth from heaven. There was no longer any desire to possess the material things that the world sought after. Nothing could compare to His presence. As she released her brother into heaven she knew it was worth it all to serve the One she loved.

*"Now it is time to touch the one I have been preparing you for. You have been in training for ten months and twenty-one days. Humbleness had to consume you to be used for this time. Just know that I will be sharing the pain you are about to experience. Every thing that is done to you is being done to me. It is the great battle against Satan's hold on this child's heart and I will come through victorious. My presence will protect you from the demons that will flee in my presence. There will be mighty angels who will form a hedge of protection around your very life. This time you cannot take your eyes off of me nor listen to any voice but mine. I have saved his life from the pits of death nine times and brought him to you so that I can claim him as my own. In the end he will know why I used you. No one else could reach him where he was. Trust me to be exalted and heal the last chains that have bound you for years. I did not come just to touch his life but to touch yours, too. The healing I will do will also heal the hearts of your children. Each one will begin a new walk with me and realize my greatness. There is nothing I can't accomplish through those that serve me. I have fine-tuned your hearing to know my voice from all others. The times you will want to give up remember the great victory that will be won from your obedience. It will be worth it all in the end though it will look like a disaster at times. It will require you to trust me completely without any reserve knowing that I am in full control."*

Mercy pondered the message for a while. She knew that His ways were perfect but it sounded so big to her. She was still not sure whom she would be helping but it must be someone she had spent time with in the past. If there was going to be that much pain she would have to trust Him completely to overcome the evil one that would be the advisory. She knew this battle would not be hers at all. It was too big for anyone but God.

Suddenly she knew who it was. He had called her ten months ago unexpectedly. She had asked him to run away with her without planning to say such a thing. Over the months he had called and they had finally agreed to meet and spend their time together away from their homes. She became excited but apprehensive because this was no small challenge. It had not worked before and she couldn't reason what would be the difference now. She wondered if her Daddy was really going to do a miracle or was this hidden desire something she had held for years. There were so many ties between them maybe it would be a miracle for both of them.

# The Greatest Calling

Mercy closed the door to the past and drove to meet the one she had loved for so many years. Even though he had been gone the love had not died in her heart. She had known all of those years he was absent in her life that he would be back and rekindle the flame. True love can never vanish if it is a love planted by God's hands. It had been so long since they had been together she wasn't sure how their hearts would be bound back together as one. The only thing she did know is that if God put them back together He could take care of every detail. With that thought in mind she drove up to her love and their new beginning.

She didn't see the wrinkles and the graying hair. As their eyes met she only saw deep into his heart. It felt as if she had been to the grocery store and just gotten back home. The empty years were not there between them. All that she felt was that she was where she belonged. The past thirty years being apart from Ron were forgotten as Mercy reached out to touch his life.

*"I did not bring you here to test you. I brought you here to fill his loneliness and be an extension of my love. It will take some time for Him to see my goodness in you because he has not been with anyone that I could shine through and touch him. You must trust*

*me to do my perfect work in his life. You are the hope he had lost to touch life to the fullest and know its meaning. He will learn that nothing else matters but the power of my presence. He has longed for peace all of his life but could never grasp its presence. I will help him to let go and let me be God to him like I have wanted to all of his life. You will be his prayer warrior and suffer many insults from his lips until he surrenders to me. Those insults represent the pain he has carried for many years."*

*"Never forget what I have told you so that you will not give up nor take offense in what he says and does. He has run from me so many times and then searched for me without surrendering to my presence. You will be the one to show him my goodness and I will display my love to him through you. When he attacks you with words that hurt and you just pour out your love to him in return he will see my glory. This must happen for him to know that I love him just like he is. My love is unconditional and pure. I long to have his heart and you are the one that will make it possible. What I am asking of you requires you to trust me without question. I will never leave your side and will show you the way. My timing is perfect in every one of my children's lives and your obedience will produce the harvest for him that I have been longing for him to enjoy. Now spread your wings and fly with my wind beneath you to carry you along and my presence to reach out from you to touch him completely."*

He could barely walk and the pain was almost unbearable. The doctor said it was a damaged nerve and would take time to heal. Mercy took care of him with gentleness and love. She cooked him healthy meals and they talked for hours about the past. As he talked she saw the loneliness in his eyes and knew he had many scars that would become beauty marks in his life.

His body healed and he became full of life again. Those in his past had used him and there was a wall of distrust that he had built around his heart. He would accuse her of faults in her past and she would hear her Daddy whisper "you were forgiven many years ago. He will learn to see my forgiveness."

There was a terrible fear within him that she would only love him again if he gave her money. He would repeat many times a day that he was broke. The good thing was that she didn't want his money she wanted his heart to trust her. She would talk to her Daddy every night and tell him she didn't want to be a bum and appear she had nothing in life. She felt ashamed of being poor and dependent and wondered how anything positive could ever come out of their union.

*"You must trust me completely. Even though it appears that your life has amounted to nothing I will take the veil off of his eyes that he might see the importance of life. If I had brought you to him with money he would have never been able to understand how great I am. I take the lowly to touch the hearts of the rich in material things so that the rich might see what they must have to serve me. Did I not tell the rich man to go and sell all that he had and follow me? He walked away thinking he must be poor to serve me. If he had asked me I would have told him that I multiplied back twice as much to Job as he had before because he obeyed me. I must require that a child of mine let go of anything that is first in their life so that I can be first to them. When they let go of things that are of this world then I can bless them with riches from heaven. When they see my glory upon the weak and poor then they begin to understand what brings peace into their life."*

*"You must walk in peace and loves no matter how many times others condemn you. I have many treasures here on earth for you but there is a time for everything and now is not the time. Who can question how and when I bless them for no man is worthy of my goodness. It is only because of my mercy and unconditional love that I can bless whom I choose to bless at any time. The world does not understand mercy and grace because of their hard hearts and sinful nature. To obey me is one of the greatest sacrifices I will ever ask of you. My ways are not the ways of the world and you will not*

*understand what I am doing at the time I ask. Later you will see that I can accomplish my perfect will through those who listen to my voice and obey me."*

*"If you will wear the cloak and not take it off I will do miracles through you. There are so few that can keep the cloak of humility on. It is the cloak you wear that will bring my son home to me. All of the tears that you will cry for my sake will wash the veil that is on his eyes and set him free. Someday your children will know why I sent you to him. See the light that is shining in the distance? It is the victory after the storm that I have won. Take courage now and let us move on."*

The bashing of her character began and Mercy remained silent presenting no defense. Every detail of her past was cast before her daily and she silently reminded herself that she had been cleansed from all sin and been forgiven. At least once an hour he reminded her that she never knew how to handle money and that was why she was poor. In the same sentence she was told she wanted to live rich and run with the wealthy. She was judged daily and she knew it was Satan trying to steal her cloak that her Master had placed upon her. Confusion was a constant presence accusing her of being lavish and then stating she had nothing because she didn't know how to plan. As the taunts became worse Mercy drew closer to her Daddy. She knew He was in control of the situation but wondered if she should speak up and defend herself. One day her Master came and told her many things she did not understand.

*"The accusations against you are really the guilt he feels from his past. He sees that you have changed and knows the dark side of him that is not of me. The demon holding him down is called pride. If he confesses he is wrong and wants to serve me he will be made weak in your sight. He is like the rich man that refused to give up everything to follow me. In time he will learn that becoming weak sets man free to follow me. Pride carries many companions with him. Jealousy, envy, and control stay close to pride and try*

*to consume everything in their path. They are never satisfied and cause man to self-destruct in the end."*

*"I can only reach my children through divine intervention through the ones that obey me. Few choose to be obedient because they don't understand my ways. When he is the most resistant is the time he will be the closest to bowing before Me so rejoice in the darkest hour know many miracles in his life are at hand. Only by wearing the cloak will he be able to learn my character and great love for him. Peace is the constant companion of humility and my peace is the greatest gift I have for man. Let me hold you now and give you rest."*

*"I brought you to Brady to tell your story to the world. The office for insurance is my office to send out a message to the world. Think it not strange that the very computer you are writing my words from was bought by the man who must be set free. Your kindness and gentleness has set him on fire and only I can distinguish that fire. The great battle in his life has been won and you will see the victory soon. Don't be discouraged for you will soon see my glory in this situation."*

Every day felt like the darkest hour in Mercy's life. The controlling spirits soon became outlandish and covered with confusion. She reached the point she didn't want to eat the food of such a foolish man. Every time the spirits got stronger her Daddy would send her to Austin where she would spend time in prayer and become refreshed with His peace.

Her granddaughter Trin would cover Mercy with love and hold her tightly. The love from Trin's eyes sparkled so brightly tears would roll down Mercy's face in gratefulness knowing a child's love is pure. He refused to acknowledge Trin knowing that she gave strength for Mercy to keep trying to live. He taunted the small innocent child knowing she would react. When she asked him to stop he would say she was bad. Trin would always tell Mercy when she left to remember she would always be in her heart.

When Mercy would return to him she was greeted with anger and resentment. She was told she had left to go drinking and partying. Each time she returned the condemning spirits grew stronger. Because she had spent money on gas to go to Trin she could not have anything but food. She said she needed a haircut and was told the little dog needed one worse and his didn't cost as much. Mercy said no more and cut her own hair. Actually, her Daddy cut her hair. It was the best cut she had ever had and looked professional. She had no money to buy special scissors so she used a pair of dull scissors that she had found.

Clothes were not an option so her daughter gave her clothes to wear. Her shoes wore out and her children bought her more not knowing how badly she really needed them.

The shattering of her heart continued and she remained silent. She knew she had to remain stable to change the life of the one she had been sent to help. Material things no longer had any meaning to her as she realized that her Daddy always met her needs.

Soon she began crying everyday for her Daddy to take her home to Austin. The only way she could survive this great task was her solitude alone with God.

Each day brought a new set of obstacles that were overcome with humility. Deep in her heart she knew her Daddy would provide. Every month when the house payment came due it was there. She could never explain to anyone where it came from because it came from the strangest ways. She knew her Daddy had told her the house that He had given her was paid for so she had no choice but to wait for it to come His way.

When she had no gas money her son gave her a gas card. It was used to travel to Odessa to take care of Sarah, her granddaughter. She also drove to Cleburne often to work for Kim and Kent.

Mercy's make-up ran out and her younger son, Casey, bought her more. It enhanced her wrinkles so badly she gave it to her granddaughter, Randi. Kim found out and gave her best make-up money could buy. God seemed to always be a step ahead to provide her with all of her needs.

She would lie awake at night thanking her Daddy over and over for taking such good care of her. As she cried with sadness in her heart she saw Him catch her tears in His hand and hold them to His face. What a loving God she served as she awoke each day wrapped in His sovereign love. It seemed never ending but she knew He would win the victory He so desired.

The wedding was coming soon. Her youngest daughter was getting married and oh, how Mercy wanted to share the experience with her. Unexpectedly she had to go to Austin to check on her house. It was the very day her daughter was going to find her wedding dress. Mercy got to go with her and it was such a special time. She had no money to buy it but her daughter knew and understood. There was no money to buy the mother's dress either. She knew that she would have one some way so she just waited.

When Mercy returned home he would not speak to her for two days. She stayed at her office during lunch and spent time in prayer. She was accused daily of running off to Austin to get drunk and chase men. At that point Mercy began to laugh to herself. She did not ever get drunk and she certainly never wanted to chase men. Her main man was God and He was all she wanted. Then he told her she would have to sell insurance in Odessa because that was where the most money was.

Mercy applied for every job she could find on the Internet and she got no response. She begged her Daddy to give her work and it never came. Finally, one day in desperation she knelt down by the office chair and began crying. She asked God to please let her know she was where she should be. She told Him that she couldn't take the abuse anymore. As she waited for Him to come she began to feel His awesome presence enter the room. Then she felt the peace she loves so much.

*"I have not left you nor forsaken you. I see where you are my child. Even as he tortures you it touches me, too. You have been in an emotional prison for my sake and I will free you soon. This is his last chance and we can't quit now until I reach him. I feel your pain and agony when you feel it and I will never let it destroy you. There will be many who will not believe what you have been through for my sake but those are the ones whose hearts are hard. The world will never understand what is demanded of the ones who follow me. They would rather use the word "luck" when I bless you and "you brought it on yourself" when things are bad for you."*

*"My greatest commandment is love and the world is full of hate and jealousy mixed with greed and envy. You will be labeled a failure for following me but when I pour out my blessings on your life they will call it luck. They will seek you for answers to get blessings like I have given you but they will not be willing to pay the price. The price is too high for their worldly nature. In their eyes weakness to me is a sign of failure but without weakness I cannot make you strong with my spirit. In their mind humility is weakness and they will not humble themselves to me."*

*"From now on I will let you see the demons on others so that you might understand their bondage. When you pray for them I will answer and when you speak to the demons they will flee. They are not afraid of you but hate my presence. They know I can destroy them at any time and flee in terror at the sight of my almighty power. This is why my anointing must stay on you at all times. As long as you wear the cloak you will have my anointing. When we get to the travel trailer where he is you will begin to see what I am saying and learn how to drive them away."*

Mercy rose from the chair with a new strength. The fears and helplessness were gone and she was ready for warring in the spirit. As she approached the trailer she saw a buzzard circling it. Her spirit recognized it was the signal for "the kill" of his spirit. She commanded the demons to leave in the name of Jesus and the buzzard disappeared into the sky. She was ready to enter the battle zone.

She entered the house and saw him sitting in the chair looking almost lifeless. The demon of pride was grasping his neck tightly and it was huge. On top of pride a smaller demon of greed clung to his hands and held him prisoner. The chains looked huge but were loose enough he could easily slip his hands from them. Jealousy jumped out of his body and circled Mercy as she entered the room.

When she came closer to him the presence of His anointing caused the demons to scream and run in every direction. He slumped down as if released from the heavy weight that had been on him.

She began to pray silently for the Holy Spirit to minister to him and peace filled the room. Mercy knew this was the beginning of his healing and she held him close in silence. As she held him she saw him looking in front of her toward the door. There stood the demon of pride trying to hide by the door. As Mercy looked toward the door the demon flew outside and began looking in the window by him. He clutched his pants pocket with one hand and a demon of greed wrapped himself around his hand.

Suddenly she saw the house was full of angels so tall their heads touched the ceiling. They surrounded her and stood at full attention with their faces looking upward. His presence fell at that moment and thousands of demons flew out of the house in every direction. This was the first time she had come home and not been attacked verbally when she entered the door.

Mercy knew she had just been in the center of a spiritual battle. The angels had their arms raised and was praising God singing the most beautiful songs she had ever heard. She sat still and listened as they sang. He sat across the room from her with his eyes closed.

She wondered if he could hear them singing. She knew now that she couldn't give up no matter how many battles she would face.

*"The battle is not yours, it is mine. That was not the last battle but it was the one that destroyed the wall around his heart. I have much work to do in his life in a very short time so trust me to accomplish my perfect will for him. Soon he will begin longing for my presence he felt today and will yield to me. Your suffering will be worth it all as you escort him into my kingdom. He is past the point of permanent rehabilitation in my ways so I must move quickly and claim him at the right moment. You will understand more as you see me moving in his life."*

*"His mother asked me to save his life and that is what I am doing now. He has run from me so many years and is only now ready to rest in my presence. Satan knows this and is fighting for his very soul. He will wait until the next opportune time and will attack again. He will not curse you today because of the peace but tomorrow he will resort to his old nature because he has not learned to trust me. I will show you more as you can handle it so be content now knowing that I am in full control of this situation."*

Mercy rested the remainder of the day in peace and was not attacked in any way. He was kind and considerate unlike all the days before. His spirit was free and he laughed and joked with her. She knew he had tasted the goodness of God and would want more of Him in the future. She also knew tomorrow would be a new day and she would have to stand strong again in the spirit of her Master.

As the day of the wedding approached he became more irritable. He informed her that it had nothing to do with him and he didn't care. She knew he was feeling insecure and did not respond to his attitude.

Her plan was to take two of the granddaughters with her a few days early to prepare. She had not gotten a dress and had only a little time left. He gave her money for gas and told her she would need to buy the older granddaughter's dress if she asked her to do so. There was just enough to buy her granddaughter's dress, gas, and spend $30 on a formal mother's dress for herself. She knew her Daddy would give her a beautiful dress no matter how little she had to spend. She found that dress and it was so beautiful everyone thought she had spent a fortune for it. She found it in the second store she went in and spent only two hours shopping for everything. What a great God she served. He had not given her any extra for a wedding gift but that day she sold enough insurance to give them money they really needed for their bills. God's almighty hand was there for every day she was gone. He had provided not only for her needs but also for the tiniest desires of her heart.

She entered the door and he rushed out with their granddaughter headed for Odessa. He was going to take her home and spend the week there. He threw just enough money at her to buy gas to get to Cleburne to work for her daughter and son-in-law. She felt abandoned but yet set free. At least she wouldn't be told daily that she didn't know anything.

She left quickly to spend time with her Lord. When she got there her children loved on her and made her feel special. They had bought her a beautiful purse that was very expensive. She had walked through the stores many times wondering if she would ever get to carry a purse like that. She had never told anyone but God knew. He also knew that Ron would go through her old purse frequently to see if she had anything in it he did not know about. She never confronted him on this because she had nothing to hide. The love of her children covered her as she spent time with them. They laughed and loved on each other all night. They couldn't know the prison she was in because she knew that someday soon she would be set free.

*'There are still more battles to come. We will spend this week together and I will fill you with my strength to conquer the enemies*

*of his soul. This week he will be alone and all of the demons from hell will taunt him and attach themselves to him. You will go to him in Odessa at the end of the week and I will fight a great battle to set him free. He will not be set free until you reach the travel trailer where he will be willing to be set free. I give man freedom of will to make choices and that is why the battle will be intense. Fear not for I will win but it will be done through your obedience to my instructions. He will try to make you fall but I will lift you up and exalt you before his very eyes. He will be in awe at the greatness of my power in your life. There will be so many demons attached to him that they will try to attach to everyone near, even his son. The only thing you need to remember is to stand still and see my glory as I win a great battle in his life. There is no way you can prepare for this except by spending time with Me and listening to My voice."*

*"The enemy will try to mimic my voice so you will spend this week learning to recognize my voice above all of the others you hear. I speak truth and confirm what I tell you. He will speak lies and your spirit will sense the difference. He will try to use your emotions and I will always move your spirit in a knowing that it is I. This week I will fine tune your hearing and obedience to claim a great victory so stay alert and do not give up."*

She loved the quiet and peacefulness at the ranch. Her spirit was free to worship Him with all of her heart. She spent time with Him and told Him all of the deepest secrets in her heart. Sometimes she caught herself smiling as her heart was poured out before His throne. The most beautiful times were when she just worshiped at His feet and gave her love to Him. It was wonderful because He never criticized her and understood her heart. He was her comforter and best friend. Mercy longed to stay here forever but she knew she had to move on to accomplish the Father's will.

He called and accused her of someone being with her there. He said she had lied about not having a phone at the ranch. He told her the ball was in her court and she had to make up her mind what she wanted. She was accused of everything he could think of but when she tried to call him he never answered. He said he was outside working and couldn't hear the phone. Then he said he couldn't get any work done because it had been raining. She realized that now not only did she have to deal with the accusing spirits but with lying spirits and malice. The devil wanted to play games and she was not willing to play in his court. She would not bow to evil and she would not play their games. She knew the battle was in full force and she would have to listen closely to the One who led her through the fire. She didn't care how high the flames got she would not play their game.

Mercy rode to Odessa with her daughter and new son-in-law. It was such a wonderful trip hearing about their honeymoon and all the funny things that had happened. She let go and laughed and enjoyed the trip knowing what would lie ahead. No one could take this tiny bit of joy from the day and she cherished it in her heart.

He came to get her at her son's house and brought the little dog with the expensive hair cut. She wasn't envious of the dog but felt belittled at how little her needs were noticed. As she watched she noticed the dog had the same personality as the man did. When someone tried to pet the dog he would growl. Then he tried to attack her son's dog that looked at him like he was crazy and walked away. She knew this would be a battle this weekend and steadied herself for the battle ahead. He began telling their son that they couldn't go out to eat because he had spent too much money on her trips to Austin.

He reminded her on the way to his house that it cost a lot of gas to come get her. Then he told her that he knew she had spent all of the money he had given her because she had never learned to handle money. She secretly wanted to slap him but restrained herself and remained silent. She saw the demons on him and they were dancing in glee as if they had won a victory. She silently told her Daddy to confront them and run them off. He told her to command them to leave and they would go. She ordered them to leave and they flew everywhere out of the truck. When they got to his house she saw them perched so thick you could not see the roof. Mercy clutched the cloak close and held her head high. They could not steal her spirit or her service to the Master.

They entered the house and it was dark and smelled like soured water. The house was empty except for a few pieces of worn furniture. There were no sheets, towels or washcloths in the house. There was no hot water and very few lights. What a perfect place for the demons to roam and they were having a party. They were every size and as she walked around they began to scatter frantically. One screamed and told her to get out but she just smiled and kept walking around with the authority her Master had bestowed on her for this time. He stammered and tried to talk but could not complete a sentence. She had never experienced anything like this and was ready to fight. Everything became quiet and peace covered Mercy in the midst of the storm.

The next morning Ron went with a friend and she took the truck to go to Justin's house. She stopped at a convenience store and they were there. His friend said he had sold a car for Ron and handed the money to Mercy. She decided to give it to Ron later.

That afternoon he came to pick her up. He told their son he would have the corvette he owned worked on and he could come and get it. It seemed as if he was reminding her that she had no car of her own because she couldn't handle money. She really didn't care what he thought because she had used what she had to help her children. She had bought them cars and given them money for years. She had been a giver and not a taker.

When they got to his house he told her she needed to decide if she was going to move to Odessa. He started ranting about what she should do and said she couldn't survive anywhere else. She placed the money on the table beside of him and went to bed. Mercy did not want anything from him except his love and instead she was beaten down daily by his words. The thing that bothered her was why he wanted her to be a failure. She had worked hard for many years and encouraged others even when she was down. She whispered to her Daddy that she couldn't take it anymore. There was no reason for anyone to be belittled every day for no reason. She decided to go home. She wanted to go home to the home God had so graciously given her that was filled with peace.

As they started back to Brady he began to taunt her again. He told her that she was negative and had a chip on her shoulder. She did not respond but wore sunglasses to hide her tears. When he asked if she wanted to stop and see their oldest granddaughter she said she just wanted to get to Brady.

He said she had been mean to her mother many times and never apologized to her. It was so cruel for Mercy to hear those words. He knew she had carried guilt about her not having the chance to tell her mother she was sorry before she died.

It felt as if the gates of hell had been loosed upon him and were using him to attack her very being. She knew she couldn't take it anymore. She asked her Daddy to please take her home to Austin and deliver her from this prison.

*"I will not allow his abuse much longer. This is his last chance to enter my kingdom and I need you to stay. The things he says about you are how he feels about himself. He knows you survived and raised the children without him and feels like he is the guilty one. Transferring blame is a tool the devil loves to use on my children. If he can convince them they are not worthy of me then the blood of My Son has no meaning. He uses every tool to cause you to give up and when you give up the victory is his instead of mine. I will never put on you more than you can bear. I will not allow this man to be the one to give you a car. It would be given with wrong intentions and with strings attached. You know he would tell you that you could never go see Ashley and could only drive what he gave you in Odessa. Right now he is walking on dangerous ground and I will not let him torment you forever for his own faults. He is*

*more miserable than you can imagine and seeks to bring you down because you want to serve me"*

*"Satan knows that I have promised you a car and he is trying to make you feel like it will never happen. Remember, he uses emotions to bring you down. I will give you a car in a most unusual way. It will be such a way that no one can say they had a part in my gift for you. It won't be some old ragged car that is worn out. It will be the best for I give the finest of gifts for my children. Because you have been patient and not complained for so long great will be your reward. Satan tells you that you have lost your dignity but I tell you it will be exalted before the eyes of every person that judged you as a failure. My timing is perfect and I will not forget my promise to you."*

The next day Mercy talked to her oldest daughter. She told Mercy she wanted to pray for her. It was such a beautiful prayer and she asked their Father to give Mercy a good car within the next week. She knew we can't make God do things in a certain time but she did know that He heard their prayer. She began thanking Him for helping her and taking such good care of her. He was her husband and much better than an earthly one. He always saved her and never condemned her.

She went to her office and wrote as her Daddy directed the words of her life. God spoke and she wrote and continued to write every day.

She asked her Daddy to have the man he had sent her to help quit criticizing her and even quit cursing everything he thought about or saw. A change in him was happening and she was so glad to be released of the accusing spirits. They would be in the house when she first got there each day but they scattered as she entered the doorway. She knew they were waiting for the next opportune time to attack but she stood firm in His anointing.

Ron told her he wouldn't go anywhere that he could not control the situation. He didn't like Austin because he had no control there. In Odessa he could control everything because it was his own place and it was paid for. He said he couldn't afford the gas so he would ride back with a friend to Odessa and she could come when she was ready.

*"You will not be a prisoner in his home. He does not know it but he is not in control of your life and he is not in control of this situation. Man can make all of the plans he wants to but I will have my way. I am your Master and you will follow me. If he does not choose me to be his Master he will be left alone without me. His days are numbered and I must speed up my work in his life. Do not fear nor be concerned about what I do for my way is perfect and no man can control me. It is the demon of pride that seeks to control everything in life. Confusion has filled his mind and convinced him that you will take his money. Deceit has convinced him to protect himself from you by constantly repeating that he has no money. He has been filled with deceit and lies have become his best friend. He is still running from me and is frantic. He knows if he bows to me he will not have control of his life. To obey me would mean that he would have to be released of all of the demons and he thinks his lies would be uncovered which would cause him shame. What he doesn't understand is that lies demand more lies and deceit has a permanent residence in his life. I can present myself to him who will cause the demons to flee but he has the freedom of choice to invite them back."*

*"You will never understand the reasoning in his mind to see you with nothing because it is his punishment transferred to you. Confusion chants to him that if you fail his children will believe all of the lies he has said about you will be true. It will prove that you don't know how to handle anything and you caused your own failure. I will exalt you before his very eyes and prove him wrong. This is the only way the deceit in his heart will be exposed. When he asks me for forgiveness I will heal him and bring him home to me. Deceit is too*

*familiar a spirit to him and he cannot tarry when he repents. Trust Me in this and I will bring it to pass quickly."*

Mercy knew that the wonderful things He had spoken to her would come to pass. It would be a miracle that only God could do. She also knew there would be more traumas ahead until the final round.

He called everyone he knew and told them he would be in Odessa soon. She heard him tell one woman that he would check out a place to start a new café there. He told her it was for rent but that he could probably buy it. He also said he would repair his house and sell it. Then he would buy a used pickup and travel trailer and live in it. Never once did he say "we" but it was always "I". This reassured Mercy that she would never have to live in Odessa again.

Her car lost antifreeze so often she had to refill it almost every day. He told her that he would buy her a new cap for the radiator and that should solve the problem. In other words he was telling her that she might as well accept she would never have anything to drive but a borrowed car. Mercy knew differently. She and Kim had prayed and she knew what God had promised her so she was not moved by his comments.

*"When you can ignore what he says and believe I will do what I said I would do then your battle is won in the spirit. When you reach the point that you stand without doubting then I will show my glory. That is called faith and to whom much is given much is expected. I expect you to have more faith than many around you because you know my voice and my power. You have done all that you can do so now you must just stand and wait upon me. Remember that I told you that man can make all of the plans he wants but I will have my way. I can foil any plan and crush it before it begins. Whatsoever a man professes is what he will have and if he keeps professing that he is broke he soon will be as he says. Also understand that when the battle with this child is won there will be others that I will send you to for me to reach out through*

*you. No battle will be the same but each will require your trust in who I Am. Each time you will become stronger in me and as you grow stronger I will give you greater assignments. This is why you must wear the cloak of humility. Even when you stumble you will surely not fall as long as you trust in me. Are you ready to see my victory in this battle"?*

Mercy felt a great relief as she listened to her Daddy. She knew she was covered by His perfect work.

When Mercy told him she would be caring for Trin, he immediately loaded up some of his things and left early the next morning. As usual he made conflicting statements. He was going to clean up his place. Then he was going to look for a job because he was broke. She knew he was really going there to wait and see if she would come.

*"I have removed him for now to give you time to spend with me. I have promised that I would never put on you more than you can bare and I will keep my word. He will have time to think and I will speak to him and let him know what I want him to do. Just remember, I give man freedom to choose and it will be his choice. You are mine and I will take care of you no matter what his choice is to do. So far, he has not let go of his old life and is afraid of anything new. He wants you but is afraid you will not stay with him and doesn't want to take the chance. If you go to his place you can't make him leave. I see your weariness and will force him to decide. You have been obedient to me and I will not allow you to be in bondage to anyone. He must make his choice now for there is no reason for you to suffer anymore. There has been a lot of healing in this assignment I have given to you. You have a forgiving heart toward him and have shown him kindness and love. I will not put you back together until he decides what to do".*

Mercy didn't know what would happen but she hung on to all of the promises her Daddy had given to her. It would take a miracle to fulfill His promises but that was nothing to worry about because God was in the miracle business.

# The Interim

As the days went by Mercy walked in peace and enjoyed Trin. They played together and prayed together and there was peace. His anointing became stronger and stronger as she spent time with her Master. She knew that He was putting everything in order for her future and could hardly wait.

One night she asked Him for something she had longed for most of her life and had never received. She asked her Daddy to please let her have a husband the way one was designed to be. She wanted one that would love and cherish her and fulfill her every need. She wanted a man that would be positive and a Christian. Then she asked Him if there was such a person for her and if there were would He bring him soon.

*"I saved the best for last for you my child. There is one that has been searching for you for many years. He has often asked me to bring you to him but I had to finish my work in your life first. You would never have given your all in any relationship until you finished this chapter in your life."*

*"You have been in the desert for thirty years and I have been by your side. You have become strong and full of faith even though*

*you don't think so. Now the Promised Land is in sight and I have blessings that I will pour out upon you and set you free to run instead of walk. You will leap with joy and forget the shame of your youth. You were forsaken by all but me and I have rescued you for such a time as this. Everyone thinks you will fall but I have told you that even though you may stumble many times I will not let you fall down. You will now run the race of life with wings like the eagle. You will soar and reach the mountaintop of life and no one can take this from you. Not only will your soul prosper but also I will prosper everything you set your hands to do. Those who know you will gasp in wonder at the blessings that surround you. Others that see you will want to know what your secret is to enjoy life so fully. Your answer will be the words I put in your mouth and they will be astonished. From now on my anointing will not leave you as long as you wear the cloak of humility. I will perform my word that I have now spoken quickly and unexpectedly so be ready to soar".*

Mercy was overjoyed at the words her Daddy had spoken. She trusted Him and knew that He would bring it to pass. She also knew that it would be in His perfect timing.

One week later Ashley and Zack came to visit her and Trin for the day. They laughed and talked for hours and it was so refreshing. She had never told her children the awfulness of her situation or of her hearts cry to God just a week before. Suddenly Ashley told her she was such a beautiful woman so full of life. She told her that soon she would meet the man of her dreams that would treat her like a lady and be to her what she had always wanted. She said it would be soon and that she had done what she had been led to do for others and now it was her time to enjoy life to the fullest. Mercy couldn't believe what she had heard. She had not breathed a word about her heart's desire and it was as if God had spoken through Ashley's lips. This had to be confirmation for what He had told her only a week before. Mercy hoped it would be very soon because she was so ready for a new life.

The next morning Mercy and Trin enjoyed each other for a while and then Trin began watching a Disney movie. As she sat in His presence she heard him speak these words.

*"You know the one that I will bring into your life. You have never met him face to face but you witnessed to him and it changed his life forever. Remember the one you sent a thank you card to eight years ago? He told you that your son would reach the mountaintop and would exceed to the fullest. I told you to send him a copy of a book and mark the pages where it spoke of my choosing righteous judges to judge my people. They will look at the heart of man and I will judge through them. He is one of the righteous judges I have chosen and he knows it. Because you were obedient I spoke to him and changed his life. He has never forgotten you and has asked me many times to let him meet the one that obeyed me. Many times during the years you have thought of him and wanted to see him. He already knows your character and will always respect you for taking the time to touch his life. For many years he has searched for the right one to share his life with just as you have searched for the one I have chosen for you. He will be the one that helps your son become appointed as a federal judge. There will be many wonders in your union with him. You will soon see how I am putting together my army to overthrow the evil one. He lost the battle two thousand years ago but has refused to surrender. I will overthrow him and his army through my people once and for all".*

The revelation she had just received was so great she sat still for a while for the words to sink in. She looked over at Trin so innocent and small sitting on the sofa unaware of what He has just spoken. Her tiny arms grasped the puppy she had just gotten and she was at peace with the world. Mercy wanted more than anything to touch this child's life and make a difference in her life. Her parents worked every day and she had known day cares since she was born. This was the time she could spend time with her and teach her all that she could. She learned so quickly and never forgot what she saw and heard so Mercy knew she must make the most of this time with her. Mercy asked her Daddy to put the right words in her mouth and speak them to Trin in such a way she would never forget what was said this day. There was a reason they were together at this time and she wanted to fulfill God's purpose for this day. She asked Trin to sit in her lap and she began to tell her a story.

This was the time Mercy would spend in her final training for her Master so she carefully listened to all that he told her. He told her to go to Cleburne and spend time with Blake, Will, Sarah, and Trin while Kent and Kim worked. She saw His spirit on each one of the children and knew that He was in the midst of them.

As they started to town the last day the hood came loose on the car and the top part flew off onto the side of the road. Mercy kept driving because she knew that her Daddy had the car He had promised her almost ready. As she looked at the poor little car so torn and pitiful she realized that the material things in life are so fleeting and soon wear out and disappear. They start out new and enticing but eventually grow old and become worn beyond repair. She now understood why He said that He would supply all of our needs and did not say He would give us lavish material things. Our needs are really His spirit upon our lives that gives us life that is filled with peace no matter what we face. She could think of nothing more important now except to worship at His feet.

*"I have always supplied your entire needs child. Sometimes what you thought you needed something you really wanted to have something that someone else had. It is the intent of the heart that I look at when you make your requests to me. If your intent is to be a blessing then I give freely. If it is to compete with others I say "no" because I want to keep your heart pure."*

*"Satan will use the mouths of others to try to make you feel defeated but do not listen. You do not have to please anyone but me and I don't look at what you own but who you are and the condition of your heart. I would have you to live as if this is the last day you will be on this earth. Enjoy the life I have given you this day and do not*

*worry about what tomorrow will bring. Touch life, laugh, and taste my goodness. It is then that you will begin walking in my anointing and my power will be upon your life."*

*"Look closely and you will see my arms around you as you go through life. We will run and laugh and enjoy each other's presence. You will learn to smile when others look at you as if you have no hope. They don't know the great plans that I have for your life and they will be ashamed when they see the great miracle I will do through you. It is then they will come to you wanting to know how you did it and you will counsel them in my ways."*

*"I am warning you now that when you get to Odessa everyone will be quick to place you where they want you but I will have my way. Do not reply or dispute their plans just know that I have already taken care of everything and I will keep My promises to you."*

As Mercy, Sarah, and Trin drove to Odessa they laughed and talked about the miracles that God had done. They all held hands and agreed that God would give Mercy a good car to drive and this time they just left it to Him to pick it out and bring it to her.

For weeks Mercy and Trin drove and drove. The car that everyone laughed about took them everywhere they needed to go. She began to feel so sorry for everyone around her that had criticized and laughed at her. They had nice cars and big car payments. All the while they wanted something better and newer. They could not see the blessings they already had. They were wasting the time they could have spent with God looking for something better and newer. It was Satan's greatest tool to lure God's children with the material things in life. They got and they got and were never satisfied. She knew she must pray for her children everyday to be protected from the lures that were everywhere in life.

For the first time she could remember Mercy began taking life slower. She talked to her Daddy all day every day. She saw Him in everything she around her. She knew the anointing was growing upon her life and soon she would be covered completely. She laughed at Satan's tactics they were so obvious. At last she did not fear at what he claimed he would do to her. She knew now that the only way he would win any battle in her life would be if she surrendered and gave up. She was going to stand and believe no matter what anything looked like. She knew the tall walls that had surrounded her would fall down just like in the battle at Jericho.

Mercy was beginning to understand that sometimes her Daddy would speak directly to her heart. Other times he would speak through someone else. Everyone she talked to told her to do what would make her happy. Her happiness was serving her Master and being in His will so she began seeking Him to find His will for her life. The more He was silent the more she began to seek Him and cry out to Him. No one around her was aware of her searching for answers. She was just someone they called when they needed something and she knew it. Finally one day she turned her phone off and waited for God to tell her what to do. No one had even bothered to answer her calls so it was time to quit being a doormat. She would stand up and be how He had designed her to be in her life. She waited and listened. Then suddenly He came to her.

*"I had to get you still so I kept everyone from talking to you. If they had called you would have been trying to please them instead of waiting for me. I want you to trust me and know that I will keep my promises to you. Do you remember when you bought the house in Odessa? You had no job and could not make payments for six months. I had you march around that house once a day for six days and on the seventh day you claimed it was paid. I brought help to you and you lived in that house for sixteen years. I did that because you asked me to help you."*

*"Do you remember when I whispered to you in your closet that the house you live in is paid for? Well, Satan threatened foreclosure four times but every time I intervened and then I paid for it in full. Again, you had no job and no one wanted to help you. They told you to let it go back and they would help take care of you but they*

*didn't mean it. They were afraid you would ask them for money and if you just let go of it they would not have to give you financial help. That is the selfishness of man and I have kept your heart from being that way."*

*"The house I have given you will be used for my glory and they will be ashamed when they see how I touch many lives through you. You know how the mother with children who was abandoned by her husband feels and you care. You know how the man whose wife left him feels as if life is hopeless and he don't have the strength to find work. The ones that have no car weigh heavy on your heart because you had no car and didn't know what to do."*

*"Your youngest son gave you his extra car to drive but many times you called your children to feel their love and they never answered. That is how I feel when I call your name and you are too busy to slip away and spend time with me. You know your children love you in their own way but they don't even think about your loneliness. One of them wants you with his dad so he will take care of you but he has forgotten that his dad never took care of you. Without My help you and your family would have starved and been homeless. Secretly their dad would have gloated and said "I told you so" but I never let that happen."*

*"This day I will relieve you of taking care of him anymore. You were obedient to me when you went to him and spent time with him. He saw your forgiving heart and your kindness but refused to let go of the chains of darkness in his life. He knew he could not control you and that is why he said you couldn't get along with each other. He was sure he could manipulate you into staying with him so he could be in control. To this point in his life he had become a master at manipulation and always won in any situation. He had never met someone that gave control of his or her life to me. He has convinced himself that you have failed in life and he must teach you how to live. I came to set him free through you but he has refused me. Now I will handle him in my own way and I set you free from this assignment".*

Mercy was surprised by His words. She had thought that she must stay with this man until God took him home. She felt relief but also sadness at the hardness of his heart. She knew she had done what her Master had asked but wished that it had turned out differently. The man had told her that she never had made good choices in cars, in jobs, in spending, and everything he said to her was about something that was wrong with her. She had withstood all of the putdowns and now she was free. There were many times she had made wrong decisions but she always asked her Daddy for forgiveness and kept trying to do better.

God had her secluded from everyone and everything and she had no choice but to wait until He spoke. There were miracles in the distance and they were approaching quickly. She got the haircut she had wanted for months. The house was put in order and all of her clothes were clean and ready for whatever she was to do next. Her phone was not turned back on and she would wait until He told her it was time. She wasn't sure but it would be great because it would be from the Master's hands.

The time alone with her Daddy was heaven on earth. He spoke words of encouragement and never reminded her of her past. She knew He had a reason to cut off all correspondence with the world because there were no distractions or requests from anyone or anything.

*"I set you aside unto myself for a reason. Until now you did what anyone asked you to do and I was second in your life. Now, you will be able to obey me and I can talk to you freely. Your last touch with the world was when you tried to call everyone you knew and no one answered except your little brother. He is the loyal one and will always be there for you. You are now ready for me to bring someone into your life that is a giver and not a taker. He will love you with all of his heart and listen to you. You need to realize that when I speak to you I never remind you of your past but when others talk to you they never let it go. I encourage and they discourage you and think that this time for sure you will finally fall. I have news*

*for them. They will fall into their own pit unless they learn my ways and listen to me. Those that think they know so much will be ashamed when they begin to learn my ways. I am your resting place and nothing shall harm you as long as you stay close to me. Everyone thinks you are at the bottom because you have no car, no job and are threatened with foreclosure. Now they will see my glory in your life and look with distaste at their own life. I am your very heartbeat and you will never again remember the shame of your youth. You were forsaken by all but not forgotten by me. Now I wall begin to bless you more than you can comprehend and my greatness will shine through you."*

As His words sunk deep into Mercy's spirit she began to give Him thanks. It was a strange kind of thanks. She thanked Him for everything she had endured because it had led to His very presence. Material things were the farther from her mind and her only thoughts were on Him, the Maker of her soul. She thought of the man she had loved for so many years. He was probably sitting in the same worn out chair thinking she would fall completely at any moment. He was like the hawk waiting to swoop down on its prey. It had given up and been left lifeless. Mercy had been close to giving up many times but her hope in Him had kept her alive. She knew the only way that Satan wins is to convince someone to give up thinking it is hopeless.

She still didn't know what to do now. She only knew she must walk by faith in Him and not by what she saw around her. Nothing had changed in her surroundings but everything had changed in her heart. All fear and uncertainty were gone. She knew the best was yet to come.

As she looked out into the distance she saw her sister walking toward her. She was sixteen years older than Mercy but they had been close. Verne was smiling and ran to Mercy and hugged her. She told her that heaven was wonderful and they had watched her all of those years she had been left alone. Verne had a lot of pain at the last with her lung cancer but now she was free. She radiated

God's love and told Mercy that there was many blessings in store so begin rejoicing. The years of drought had been so long she was unsure just how great the blessings would be. Even a kind word would be great to Mercy's ears so maybe there would be many who would see the goodness of God. She didn't want Verne to leave but she said she just came to reassure her that she had never been forgotten or forsaken. Then she disappeared and it seemed like a dream although she knew it had been real.

Trin and Mercy climbed back into the pitiful little car and left for Cleburne again. This time they were at complete peace knowing good times were ahead. No longer did they have to tell everyone they knew where they were going or how long they would be gone. They were free to go about doing God's work without trying to answer to others. The past was gone and the future was waiting for them now. She saw the Promised Land in the distance and knew that God always kept His word. She was living proof that He was faithful.

When they got back to Austin there was another letter. This was the fifth time the people she was buying the house from had threatened to foreclose on her home. Every time God had performed a miracle and sent them away. They were trying one more time to take her promise from God and it was more than she could stand. She prayed. She waited and waited and got no answer. She had tried to sell the house for eight months just in case God wanted her somewhere else.

No one even made an offer and she was sure that she had heard her Daddy tell her the house was paid for her. She didn't understand why the threats to take it continued and it was not yet paid for in full. She wondered if she had heard wrong or if she had made wrong choices causing this problem to continue. She remembered that God's word said when you have done all you can do just stand. She must believe what she knew He had told her until He told her something different.

Mercy had closed down her office in Brady and knew that chapter in her life was over. She had been there to write her story and increase her faith. Maybe she had been sent there to encourage the man she had been sent to help. She knew she had done what she was supposed to do and the rest was left to God to settle in her life.

The little car had barely made it home from Brady. Something was wrong and Mercy wasn't sure what it was so she called her younger brother Donald. He was such an honorable person. He was not materially wealthy but they had been so close the last year.

Donald had left home when it became unbearable for him last fall. They had spent months talking and sharing their lives together. He had been born after her mother had died and her dad had remarried. Now his mother was in a nursing home and their dad had died years before. They only had each other and memories from the past they both cherished. He was in the same shape she was in. There was no one to go to for help or to get advice. Now all they had was each other but that was enough. Their dream was to go to Germany and look up their ancestors there. Neither one had the money to go but they had to believe it would happen some day.

Only a year before Donald had almost lost his life cliff hanging. He had promised God that he would take care of his daughter until she graduated from high school. The day had come and she was ready to go to college in Austin. He still had a six-year-old son at home and was torn as whether to leave or stay there in an unhappy place. At least Mercy and Donald were there for each other and he could always come to her home. She wanted so badly to help others and give them a place to stay when they needed it but Satan was trying to make her give up the dream that God had placed in her heart.

Donald came to the house and looked at her car. All of the hoses were leaking and the radiator had a hole in it. Immediately he told her to take his pickup and go to Cleburne to work. He would fix her car while she was gone. She was so grateful for the help and realized that God always shows up in her time of need. She would have never made it to the next town in her little car and help had come to her door. That is always the faithfulness of God.

Mercy tried to call Ron to talk to him. She wasn't sure what she should say but she must tell him not to talk down to her anymore. He had left a message while she was working for her daughter that was unrepeatable. She tried to call several times but got no answer. She knew that her Daddy had handled the situation. She had been set free and could finally live again in peace. But where would she live? God had not answered and what would she drive? She could not see any help and didn't know anything to do but wait and see God move in her life. He had always met her needs so if she no longer needed a house or car then He would have to take care of her another way.

She called her older daughter and asked for prayer. It was the most touching prayer she had ever heard and she knew that God had heard their request. The tears flowed down her face as she touched the hem of His garment. Tomorrow Donald would bring the little car back and she didn't know what to do. She had no money to get another hood and Donald had insisted on paying for the radiator and hoses.

It seemed like an eternity as Mercy waited to hear Him speak to her but she knew it had to be in His timing. Suddenly, He was there and she was in His presence.

*"I would not ever let you suffer needlessly. If you were to move somewhere else I would have moved you the first time. This is my problem because you gave it to me so quit trying to take it back. You have told Me many times that you just want My will for your life so why are you questioning what My will is for you. I spoke through your daughter's lips today as she talked to you. I told you that I would never abandon you or put you out on the street. I want*

*you to believe in me when you see nothing. As long as you trust in me I will never let you fall."*

*"Have I not removed the man you didn't want to be with and set you free? I know you would have stayed as long as I asked you to stay but I couldn't stand to see you hurt anymore. I will never let you be abused to help someone that continues to refuse my help. I have reached out to him so many times but he cannot let go of pride. He will keep falling until he lets it go. My patience is long but a rebellious spirit is despising to me. There are seven things that I hate - lying, stealing, gossip, a troublemaker, covetousness, deceit, and mocking. He does all of these things and refuses to stop. He manipulates anyone he can and boasts that he always gets what he wants. Well, he cannot have you because I have set you apart for myself and he has gone too far in his controlling ways."*

*"You are not to think that you have done something wrong or maybe should have done something different. I was in full control through the entire ordeal and it was his decision for the final outcome. He will regret what he has done but it will be too late. He has slandered you now to everyone that would listen and I say this is enough. We will leave him alone in his misery until he cannot stand himself. Put the past behind you now and let me lead you further on the road I would have you travel. Accept your freedom now and let us move forward."*

Mercy felt a big relief and was excited about her freedom. Even if she had not listened closely enough at times He had rescued her because she loved Him. He had delivered her because she had called upon His name. Now she could go on with her life but He still hadn't told her what she should do now. She didn't want to sound ungrateful, but every time she had attacks from Satan it seemed as if He waited until the last moment to intervene. He always delivered her but she couldn't understand why He didn't just move and take over immediately. After all, God was almighty and He could do anything He wanted to as long as He did not violate His own word. What was He trying to teach her in the repeated threat of taking her home? She decided to examine her heart and see if it was in line with His word.

As she tried to see into her heart all she could do was praise God just because He is God. Not for what He had done for her or what He might do tomorrow. She praised Him because He is worthy of praise. Very few people realize His pureness and power. Man is imperfect and unless the blood of Jesus covers him, he cannot enter into God's presence. It is the blood that covers the sin and it cleanses us of all wrongs. She told Him over and over how much she loved Him and to cover her with His presence. Nothing could compare to being in His presence. It is there that perfect peace is found. She realized that it must be God who would examine her heart because He is a God of truth. He judges the intent of the heart and it is better for God to be the judge than to let man judge. She would lay her heart before Him and let Him heal her now. She must stay in His presence until she was made whole in spirit, mind, and body.

Mercy waited for further instructions from her Daddy and she felt a renewing of her mind. She began to understand that He would settle things his way. He is the righteous judge and no one can manipulate Him or trick Him. She didn't know the hearts of everyone else involved in her house situation but God did. She asked Him to judge everyone involved and settle this problem completely. It was much better for God to judge than for a worldly judge to decide her fate. She had let go of everything and would accept what God decided for her no matter what He did. The only thing she could do is praise Him while the battle was in full force. The worse things got the more she praise and worshipped the One who had given her life. She repented of everything in her past and asked Him to bless the ones who had persecuted her and taken advantage of her.

It had been several days and then the man called. It was the final call. She asked him why he didn't answer his phone when she had called. He lied and said the answering machine was messed up and answered on the second ring. She told him she had left messages and asked him if he had gotten them. He said there were no messages. Then he said he had been outside most of the time but the second time she had called the line had been busy for an hour. Her sister-in-law had said he had talked forever to his brother that night. Then he called her Ms. spin master and said she should be driving a peterbilt because she couldn't drive. That did it for good. Not only was he a liar but also he had put all of the blame on her. His voice was taunting her and causing her mental anguish. She really never wanted to talk to him again but was courteous and hung up. She could never believe that her Daddy would have her live with someone like he was. This caused her to wonder if people can ever break old habits.

*"I am the only one that can change a person's ways. They must take off the old man and put on the new man. Few are willing to change. They make excuses and cast blame on others just like he blamed you. He is refusing to bow to my authority and he thinks his money will take care of him. I will let him go and not bother him anymore until he cries out to me in desperation. He is an example of how people are when they have money. They feel secure thinking they can pay their way out of anything. What they don't realize is that they cannot buy me. I am almighty and all-powerful. I could turn his money to dust in the blinking of an eye. All that matters is that you obeyed me. I will lead you other places and will never allow you to be abused. When you do not move where he is he will tell your children that it was all your decision and act innocent. They know him better than you think they do. If they blame you I will show them the truth in such a way they cannot deny it. I will expose every lie that he tells them so do not worry about it."*

The next day Ash did not answer her phone calls. She knew that Ash was upset about something. Then Zack told her that Trin had been behaving badly. Ash finally called and said it seemed like every time she kept Trin she would act badly. While Mercy had been keeping Trin she noticed that she screamed at her a lot and demanded things from her. Mercy talked to her often about respecting others and finally Trin would calm down. Then later she would suddenly do the same thing. She said her daddy screamed at her all of the time. Mercy realized then just how hard it had been on Trin to be separated from her parents. She had tried to be so big for Mercy but she had missed her new home and her mom and dad. Mercy prayed for her that she would have peace.

Oh well, at least she had something to drive. She went outside and cleaned the little car from top to bottom on the inside. Then she decided to name her since they were stuck with each other. She called her Hope. They may both look pitiful to the world but they did belong to God. She would find a job and Hope would take her anywhere she needed to go. She would have to trust her Daddy to take care of her needs and right now there were other things more important.

It seemed that everyone she knew lied except Kim and Casey. She trusted both of them but the others would tell her anything. She never confronted them when they lied. Then one day she became convicted about not saying something to them when they lied. It seemed to only cause them to become more outlandish in their lying. By staying silent she was encouraging them to continue to lie. She decided the next time one of them lied to her she would confront them. Always before she was afraid they would get mad at her. She didn't care anymore if anyone in the whole world liked her or not. She was not here to please anyone but her Daddy.

*"I see the intent of your heart and I am pleased that you will finally stand up for yourself. You are a little old for me to have to defend you wherever you go. I am always with you but I want you to stand up for yourself and be strong. No one else will do it for you. When you do then they will begin to respect you. Now they don't. They have played you like a fiddle and feel smug about controlling you. From now on I expect you to speak up with anything that you do not agree with for I have given you my mind and my heart"*

*"If you will only open your mouth I will put the perfect words into it and speak from your lips. The first time you will be amazed at what you say, knowing it came from me. Each time you stand up you will become stronger until you will have the respect of anyone that you know. Satan has held you down with fear all of your life. Now he will run scared as you stand up and take your place where I designed you to be in life. You will not play their games any more. Do not answer the man's phone calls anymore. He is just checking to see if you know what he is doing. You could never know because he will lie even when the truth sounds better. It is part of the control that he wants to have over you. If you answer he is controlling you. If you don't, you know he will accuse you of doing wrong because that is what he does. Do not give in and listen only to my voice. He will try to lure you with money because that is what he uses to control others. You do not need any money from him. I am your provider and I will not allow you to take even one cent from his hands. When you don't then his control over you is broken. Let him find another waitress like he has always done in the past. They will be quick to take his money and then he will realize just how real and true you really are. It will be too late then and that is when he will understand that he cannot buy you like he has bought his way through life."*

*"You are worth more than pure gold to me and I will not allow you to be sold to the world. When you do not talk to him you must be prepared for him to use Justin to try and break you down. Then you will really have to be strong but I will be your strength and my strength is greater than they can even comprehend. I am your Almighty Defender so do not fear what they try to do. They will have to go through me to reach you and that will not happen. Trust Me and you will be healed and set free from their control forever."*

Mercy knew that God was about to take the bondage of fear from her and set her free. She knew that tomorrow they would begin calling and become furious that she did not answer the phone. There was nothing she could say to them. That part of her life was over. After they calmed down she would talk to Justin but she would not give in to him. The bondage had been broken and she refused to go back to the chains that had held her down for years.

She went outside and began praying. His presence was powerful and she knew that He was listening. She told him she couldn't pay Kent for his Mercedes. He had offered to sell it to her but even if her Daddy gave her the money she had rather spend it on helping the poor and needy. As she told her Daddy this she realized that she had only wanted a car like that to show others she was not poor. She would have become just like them if she had bought an expensive car like that. Bonnie would be all that she needed for right now and she refused to complain.

*"You have been healed as you prayed to me. No longer do you care to impress the world. Now you are not ashamed of what you have no matter how small it looks to the world. What you have is priceless. You have my presence that will go with you wherever you go. You are not seeking the material things in this world but you are seeking me. I am found with the ones rejected by the world. Even your own family has rejected you because they do not understand that you are just obeying my instructions. Now you will be able to relate to the ones who no one cares about. I will touch them through you can set them free just like I set you free. For now Hope will take you where you need to go. When it is time a stranger will come up to you and give you a car. It must be a stranger to do this for you. If it were anyone that you know they would take the credit and boast. It will be a gift from me and no one will touch my glory. Our main concern now is to reach out to those in need. They will appear to you suddenly without warning and I will work through you to touch them. We will take this walk together so do not be afraid. You will help them just like the stranger will help you. All fear has been removed from your life so just consider this an adventure that will allow me to be glorified. You will never regret the blessings you are about to witness as I move through your obedience."*

The next day no one called her. Everyone was silent so Mercy continued to pray. Fear attacked her but she kept rejecting it. Then the oppression set in and it was so heavy she could barely pray. She sat outside praying softly. Trin saw her crying and praying and put her arms around Mercy. Together they prayed that God would move this very day. She must be close to a miracle because Satan was doing all he could to make her give up believing that her Daddy would move the mountains in her life. She needed a breakthrough and must believe it would happen. She decided to fast and pray continually until God answered.

Her older daughter called a few days later and asked for prayer. She said she was having a bad day and under oppression. Mercy cried out to God and asked Him to please move and destroy the evil one trying to steal their blessings.

Justin called and told her to let the house go back. He told her that she would never get anything from the builder and that she didn't need a house that big. Mercy informed him that she lived there. She couldn't tell him that she helped others at this time. He would never understand the compassion she felt toward the homeless and poor.

He would do anything for her to be with his dad in Odessa. She bound Satan back from using her son against her. She knew demons had been loosed in every direction to try and make her give up believing that God would help her. She asked God to send His angels to help her if no one else would.

*"I will help you child. If no one will be obedient to bring you help then I can send the angels so do not fear what it looks like to you. What Satan means for your harm I will use for your good. Pray in the spirit without ceasing and I will bring joy in the morning. You have cried tears today but tomorrow you will be dancing with joy. Satan knows I am about to pour out my blessings on you and he is seeking to devour your victory. He cannot have it. The glory is mine and he knows it. Even your own family is trying to manipulate your destiny but I am telling you that I will have my own way in your life. I heard yours and Trin's prayer and I have answered. She*

*prays from her heart like you do and I will answer when you pray sincerely I always look at the intent of the heart and if it is sincere to glorify Me I answer quickly."*

*"Just remember, time does not control me. I control timing so trust me to move in your life with perfect timing. I will rain upon your desert. I see how dry and barren your life is and my rain will be poured out upon you. See the small cloud in the sky in the distance? That is my rain and you will have showers of joy. No one can stop my rain and I will give it freely. As you are sleeping tonight I will fill you with my strength and a knowing that your prayers have been answered."*

A sweet and soft peace covered Mercy as she heard her Daddy's words. He had heard her cry and she knew that when He hears He always answers. She knew that we only run the race in life once and she didn't want to fail in keeping up the pace.

Mercy watched her small amount of money wisely but it dwindled down to nothing and she told Ash they had no food or money. Ash brought Trin food to eat and told her to ask Kim for money for gas. There was no money and no phone calls. When she needed help the most there was no one she could talk to about her situation. God would have to do a great miracle through a stranger to help her now. She should have worked all summer instead of pleasing the man in Brady. Now she didn't know what to do.

*"Do not worry child. I have promised that my children will never go hungry or begging for bread. You shall have plenty and everyone that knows you will be in awe of the blessings that I pour out upon you. I see the pain you feel because they don't care enough to see your needs. That is the way the world is and I will provide for you myself."*

*"I know the intent of your heart was to be kind and help them but they are takers and they got what they wanted so they are through with you. I remember when you asked me to be their father because*

*neither of their dad's would take responsibility for support or raising them. I became their father when you asked me to and I will always be their Father. I will discipline them for you. No matter how many people take advantage of you I want you to keep giving with the intent of your heart to help others. If they take advantage of you then I will remove you from their clutches. You are an example of my great love and if they reject you then they reject me. Sooner than you think I will draw you and Ash so close you will forget the hurt you are feeling now. I will speak to her and she will know to see you as the gentle and loving mother that you are. Trust Me in this and I will bring it to pass quickly."*

It was the day she was supposed to go to Odessa but she couldn't do it. It would be giving up her joy of life and she wanted to touch life every second that God gave her.

Then a miracle happened that took her breath away. The president of a well-known company called and offered her a counseling position that would pay more than she had ever made before. They would furnish her a new car, expense account, and she would travel. It was everything that she wanted and she couldn't contain her excitement.

Always before she had called each of her children and told them the great news. This time she went straight to her closet, closed the door, and bowed with her face to the ground. All she could do is sob and tell her Daddy how much she loved him. He was giving her everything that she wanted all at the same time. She worshipped before Him for hours with no thought of time. It was her time to shine and she was ready. If God made it possible to have the job she wanted so badly then he would help her succeed. She would be His example to the elite and wealthy in such a way that they would want the peace and surety that she had. She only had a week to get ready to go for her training in another state.

She decided to tell only Casey and Kim. They were the ones that sincerely cared about her life. She kept remembering that when

David in the bible made decisions instead of making plans himself he went straight to the throne of God. He always asked God what to do and God always answered him and gave him victory. She would spend the week before the throne room of God and seek His face. The answer would be given to her that would be right.

Trin and Mercy went to Randi's baby shower at Kim's house in Cleburne. It was such a good time and especially to see Randi so radiant in motherhood. Her teenage years had been hard but now she was the gentle, loving woman that God had designed her to be. Her entire personality had changed. She was only concentrating on being a good mother and taking care of herself. She worked and got there on time and had become so responsible. She told Mercy that she talked to God a lot and felt a peace she had never had before. Then Mercy knew that Randi had begun to serve the Daddy that Mercy served. Her child would have His covering and be led by Christ during her youth.

On the way home Mercy and Trin had a long talk. They prayed together that God would be real in Trin's home and bring a new unity that had not been there before. Ash had brought Trin plenty of snacks so even though Mercy had no money she did not worry about food. She would fast until she was given food or money to buy food for her. God would never let her down and she knew it. She had not said a word to anyone but Kim had filled her car with gas. She drove slowly and they took their time laughing and singing songs. It was a very special time because the next day Trin would be going to kindergarten and there would be little time for her to spend at Mercy's house. She would be traveling with her new job. There was enough gas to get home and when she looked in her purse there was money. Kim had put money in her purse to help her. She was taking everything day by day and she knew that tomorrow would be taken care of just like today had been.

She had told the man that she would go to Odessa after the baby shower but she couldn't do it. He had not bothered to call her for several weeks and the few times she had talked to him were terrible. He had ranted and raved about her hiding what she was doing in Austin. She just couldn't be around him anymore. It would just be wasting their time because he would never change. It was a chapter in her life that needed to be closed and it must be done now. It would take time for Justin to understand but she knew that Michelle would help him through it. When Mercy had talked to Michelle about it she had agreed that it was not a good situation and that Mercy should do what she wanted with her life. She didn't want anyone to control her and keep her broke and helpless. She wanted to work and serve God every day of her life. Unless God had a plan that he hadn't told her about then there was nothing left to do to help the man have hope.

*"The doors are closing on your past forever. You obeyed me and I am pleased with you. There is nothing else you can do to help the ones that are left behind in your past. They could have had you in their life but they refused you so I am taking you to a new place with a new beginning. You will take nothing with you but a few clothes and I will provide the rest. The ones that rent from you will take care of the home I have given you until you return. You are about to learn new things that will help you to reach the ones I want to touch and heal. They are the ones that are the hardest to reach. The ones with money and power think they can buy their way out of any situation. When they see me in your life they will want what you have. They have no peace and worry about who will try to take advantage of them next."*

*"I exposed you to the man that had money that always cried he was broke. Money was his god and you saw how he tried to lie and manipulate you to control you. The ones I am leading you to will try to do the same thing. When they see that you cannot be bought with money or give in to their power they will be in awe. You will walk with integrity and they will recognize it. Most of them have never met someone they couldn't control and they will be amazed at your purity. You will be a challenge to them and they will fight hard to overthrow you but I will win the battle every time. Remember what I am telling you now because you will have*

*to stand strong against the power of the evil one that controls their life."*

*"I will put the right words into your mouth and my spirit will rest upon you. You will teach them my ways by your actions and the words that you speak. Many of them are very intelligent but few have wisdom to discern good from evil. They will see the wisdom that I have anointed you with and want to learn what you know. Then I will begin to counsel the ones I have chosen as my own and change their life forever. There will be ones that will turn away just like the man I sent you to but when My judgment day comes they will know I came to them and they rejected Me. The ones I remove you from suddenly you will wonder about but just know that my ways are above your ways and I know what I am doing so keep going forward and don't look back. There will be a few that know me. They will join with you to help the ones that don't know me. They will also know that I sent you because they were weak and could not stand against the controlling spirits of those who don't know me."*

*"Time is short and I must reach all that I can before I come for judgment day. You will begin having a new freedom in the spirit and joy and peace will stand with you at all times. I am leading you to the promises you have been waiting for so long. The journey through the valley was long. It was training in your life that needed to be done. Just look at the beauty marks you have gotten since you first began serving me. Men in the world call them battle scars because they don't know the victories I have won in your life. They think you were destined to be poor and there is no hope. I say you are rich in every way and you were first poor to recognize my power by wearing the cloak of humility. Pride looks down on others and humility looks up to me. When you look up you will see my glory. Now let us go forward and enjoy the beauty I have planned for your life."*

As she looked around her Mercy realized that it was just she and her Daddy going forward on this journey. They had left behind the past and she could not turn back now. Life looked so new and radiant. Even though she had no material things except a home she had no fear about where God was taking her next. His promises were wonderful so she knew that good things were in store for her life. She had learned to be thankful for the material blessings but she loved the spiritual blessings more. She would start living like this was the last day she would live. She would touch life in every way she could as if tomorrow would never come. It was a new way of thinking but her life would be quality instead of quantity from now on. She had a knowing that she would recognize anything that would waste her time and not take any side roads. She would run and not walk because she had a renewed strength that urged her forward.

The training was intense and Mercy worked hard to learn everything she could. Everyone she met was well known and had powerful positions that no one questioned. They were the ones you read about in *People* and *Fortune* magazines. She watched them bark out orders and no one questioned their authority. As she met the elite she realized that she always looked them in the eyes when she talked to them. They seemed puzzled because others around them looked down or swooned over them. Their ways did not impress Mercy but she was courteous and polite. She could feel their respect for her because she was authentic and never fake in anything she did.

Mr. T. was the first well-known man she met. He even had an assistant that opened the door for him and hung up his coat in his office. He never said thank you or showed consideration to anyone near him. Mercy felt sadness well up in her heart and she knew he was one of the ones God wanted to claim as His child. She could see the depths of his heart and he was filled with loneliness. He was afraid to trust anyone because he had been taken advantage of so many times in the past. Bitterness was also there and she sensed he wanted to give up the battles he was facing in his life. She wanted so bad to reach out, hug him, and tell him how much God loved him but that was God's job to show her how to do it.

There was a sadness that covered him and she prayed silently that God would reach out and hold him in His arms. Then the strangest thing happened. Mr. T. asked her if she had a moment to talk to him. The presence of God was so strong she could hardly move as she walked to the chair to sit down. His voice was gentle and he spoke quietly as she sat down. He asked her if she could help him bring unity to his staff. They had become divided by gossip and slander and something must be done. He looked right at her and asked what she would do if she was in his position. She couldn't believe what he had said.

Mercy waited for God to speak through her lips. She heard him answer through her voice that was so gentle it was almost a whisper. She told him every morning when she first woke up she thanked God for this new day and asked Him to give her wisdom in everything she did all day long. He had never failed her yet and she relied on His wisdom to make it through each day.

There was a silence and Mr. T. looked stunned. He had always thought he could handle any situation. If someone got in his way or didn't agree with him then he just fired them and hired someone else. The turnover in his company had been terrible the last year. He had to use a new strategy but he had never heard of this before. Then he asked her to tell him what she would do if she were in his position again.

She told him they could use the wisdom God had given her today. She would have an individual meeting with each of his top managers. Each one would be given the assignment of assessing the strengths and weaknesses of each person that was in their department. Then they would use positive reinforcement to help each one become stronger in their weak areas. Instead of emphasizing their faults they should praise their strong points and work together on their weak areas. They would be spending time on becoming better employees and forget about discussing the wrongs of others around them. She told Mr. T. he should delegate more authority to those under him and quit trying to control everything because it was not possible. Then he would feel more freedom and enjoy life more. When he became stressed and short tempered everyone around him sensed his mood and a negative atmosphere developed throughout the entire office. He was their example and like it or not his attitude became their attitude.

Everything she told him made sense and it was a real eye opener. Just minutes before he was ready to fire everyone in the office and get a new staff. Now he realized how damaging that could have been. All of the experience and training would have been lost and production would be slow to recover. He had never talked to God in his life except to say the standard prayer in church occasionally. God was just a name to him that people talked about instead of talked to. He wanted to ask Mercy how to talk to God but didn't want her to know he had never done such a thing.

Mercy knew what he was thinking and she told him to just talk to God like He was his best friend. Tell him everything he thought and felt and soon God would answer and he would know He was real. Mercy knew he hungered for a friend he could trust and she told him that when he talked to God he could be trusted completely. A true friend is loyal and God was her true friend and wanted to be his friend, too.

The seed had been planted and she knew God would do His work in Mr. T's life. She had just witnessed the miracle of her life. A man who thought he had it all needed the most important thing there was and she had introduced him to her Master. She could never tell anyone about this using his real name because he was so well known. Anyway, this was God's business and she was just His helper. Only God could change that man's life and she knew it was going to happen. He could never buy this miracle God just gave it to him freely.

Mr. T. stood up and took her hand. He thanked her for her advice and asked if she would talk to him again sometime. She told him she would be happy to visit with him anytime and it was a pleasure to talk to him now. Then she left with a bounce in her walk. She had just witnessed God touching someone that had always been untouchable. There was nothing greater than to be used by the almighty God.

Then Mercy met the next challenge. He was so much like the man she didn't want she wondered if they were twins. His words were cunning and dripping with compliments. His heart was cold as ice and his only goal was to win people's hearts. When they trusted him he would walk away laughing to himself that he had fooled one more person. He looked at the gentleness of Mercy and thought she would be easy to overcome. He didn't know that she had been almost duped by someone just like him only a few months ago. His tactics were so obvious to her she knew how to handle the situation. He was a taker like every other man she had met this far except for her son Casey. Casey was the only one that never thought about taking anything from anyone. She knew the manipulation would be something he had worked on for years. She asked her Daddy to cover her with His presence to cause the demons to leave this man while in her presence. The minute she went into his office he became speechless. He stuttered and she could see he was having a hard time thinking of what he wanted to tell her. Everyone had warned her of his ways but she knew God's ways were greater than this earthly human who had used people all of his life. His name was Mr. R. and he emphasized his importance. He tried to talk to Mercy but it was like his mind had gone blank. He stammered and said uh so many times she looked at him in wonderment. Then he asked her what it was about her that was so captivating. Joy leaped within her as she looked him in the eye and told him she was genuine in everything she did. She told him that she was there to help him and wanted to know how he needed help.

Mr. R. had never asked anyone for help in years. He didn't know how to respond to her question. No one knew that he needed someone to help him make the most important decision of his life about his company. Pride rose up within him and urged him to tell her he didn't need help from anyone but desperation for help forced him to talk to her. He asked her to please step into his office and he would explain some things to her. She saw the inner battle within him that contemplated appearing to be in full control of everything. She looked at his bent shoulders and knew he was fighting a raging battle he couldn't control.

Mercy prayed that her Daddy would speak through her and reach this man that needed His help so desperately. As she walked slowly to the chair to sit down she told him suddenly that he was not alone. At that second loneliness fled out of the room and he sighed as if a big bolder had been taken from his shoulders. He asked her how she knew what was bothering him and she sat silent for a few moments as he looked at her with anticipation.

She told him that God loved all of His children so much that He passed his love through her to touch his life and set him free of fear. She asked him to let go of fear so he could be set free of the strife that constantly gripped his heart. One tiny tear trickled down his cheek and he bowed his head. He told her that he had always been afraid to talk to God because he might take all of his material possessions away from him. Then he told her he would give everything he had to have the confidence and peace that she portrayed. The most profound Godly love flowed from her heart as she told him that spiritual blessings were worth it all and if he would just let God love him he would possess the presence of God. It was so beautiful and powerful he would never be obsessed with the things of this world again. He asked her if she would pray for him and she took his hands. She asked God to be so real to him that he would never again doubt how much He loved him. She asked for peace to cover him and for Godly wisdom to consume his being. The prayer was so powerful Mr. R.'s hands shook and he didn't move for the longest time. Finally, he raised his head slowly and thanked Mercy for her time. She moved silently out of the room and rejoiced that one more had been introduced to the One who had created this man who thought he was god. She knew that he was so hungry to have the peace that only God can give and he would never turn back now. If she never saw him again she knew he would have God's wisdom to change everything in his life for the better.

*"Do you see why I need your help with the ones that no one tries to reach? The poor and helpless do not cling to pride and they are much easier for me to claim as my own. The rich and powerful are the ones that think they don't need me. They do not realize that it is I who gives them the power to get wealth. Sometimes I take away their wealth to reach them and other times like today I reach out through my children to touch their lives. It is not my desire to take everything away from my children. I long to bless them and walk with them but if they do not listen I will do whatever is needed to reach them."*

*"You do not know much about Mr. R. except what you have read about him. The world thinks he has a perfect life and lacks nothing but he was to the point that he had nothing left to live for. His wife had asked him for a divorce and his children will not talk to him. Now I can show him how to repair the relationship with his family and enjoy life, as he has never known it before. I had been preparing him for this moment for years. My perfect timing never fails."*

*"Now maybe you can understand better why some prayers are answered even while you are praying and others take a lot of time. I have to put everything together in such a way that it is received when I reach out and touch someone. There will always be someone for me to send you to so stay close to me as we continue to reach out to my children."*

*"The last one I am sending you to is the man who would not receive you. You will write him a letter and close the door on your relationship with him forever. You will not look back and you will never enter that door again. I gave you training and you have touched the lives of the most powerful people in the world. This*

*time you will touch one who is the hardest to reach. He will have to deal with me now because you will be out of the picture."*

Her Daddy didn't have to tell Mercy who it was. It was the man she had tried to help for many years and he had never received her. She waited and then her Daddy dictated the words to say to him. She had dealt with the pain of forty-two years and God was giving her strength to close the door forever. She wrote the following letter and immediately took it to the mailbox and let go of him forever.

Dear Ronald,

I have been in much thought and decided I must write this letter to you. I hope you will have an open heart to what I tell you.

You do not know the real me. You have never tried to know me. You look back at the past when we were young and judge me on my past mistakes. I have closed the door on the past. I have forgiven you and myself for all the things we did wrong and I hold no grudges. I look at you as someone who desperately wants to be loved but you don't know how to receive it because you think someone is out to get you.

I came to stay with you in Brady to love you and take care of you. You stayed on the defensive and thought I was after money. If you will think about it I never received anything from you for years, not even enough child support to provide for our children. I am not resentful or bitter, that is your loss and not mine. The kids know the real you and they love you anyway. I love you but cannot live with you because you will never let the past go. God changed my life when you left me and He has to work on me daily but I try to do my best to serve Him. I want you to know Him like I do. Then you don't have to worry because He takes care of everything in your life.

You make me feel like a bum or taker and I am not so I will not be coming to Odessa. If you will quit trying to control and manipulate people you will have peace and begin to see good in the world. I will pray for your peace daily because I do love you deeply but for now it must be from a distance.

To this point you have never loved me with your heart. You want me for what you can get from me. I am closing the door to our past forever beginning now and I know someday God will bring someone into my life that will love me and cherish me because I have so much love to give. Love should be giving and receiving not taking. I want to share my life with someone who loves life and will love all of my children the way I love them.

Casey is the most precious child there could ever be. He is one of the only people I know personally that has the integrity of my dad, Marvin Eckert. He has no deception, manipulation, or negative in his heart and he will be a leader of our country some day. Not only that he will never compromise his integrity for the world. You need to look at him because he is my role model.

May God bless you and I pray you will spend time with Him so that you will have peace and His blessings.

I will always love you,

J

After she had written the letter Mercy felt the most powerful peace surround her. She knew that now her Daddy could move freely in her life because all of the chains of darkness from the past had been broken off of her life. The bondage she had lived in for years was gone and she had been set free.

A new excitement rose within her because she knew there were great and mighty things ahead from her Master's hands. She ran to the closet to worship and adore Him. Then He came and spent time with her.

*"I am about to move in your life like a mighty whirlwind. You have finally cleaned the room in your heart that had been hidden for so long. I will fill it now with a new beginning of love and joy that you have never experienced before. You now have a new freedom in the spirit that will be so strong it will touch everyone that I send you to touch."*

*"You will no longer be a recruiter for the company you work for now but you will be a recruiter for heaven. I placed you there to train you and now you will be used by me. You are ready to meet your soul mate and the two of you will touch many of my children in the government. There were only a few I could touch through you in the business world but there are many I desire to reach in the public offices of this country. I will send you in to break off the greed and laziness that has taken over the land I have kept free for so many years. Corruption has set in and it has become so bad even infidelity no longer is shameful to the world. The reason there has been no discipline to the ones that had affairs is because all of the others had been guilty of the same offenses and were afraid they would be found out if they took action."*

*"I will go in and clean my house of law in the land and replace the ones who refuse my integrity. I will give them the chance to change and they must decide to serve the world or me. If they do not choose then I will remove them quickly and replace them with My Godly servants who know me. Time is short and I am putting an end to deception that has swept the world. My blessings have been on the USA since the beginning and I have kept her freedom. Now I will touch the ones who will be willing to serve me and anoint them with my integrity. Do not be afraid of who I send you to because it is I who will speak through your lips and accomplish what I have set out to do."*

She knew it could be this very day or it might be several months because her Daddy does not wear a watch. She was determined to be led by His spirit and trust Him to take care of her each day. As she reminisced on the past to make sure she had let go of everything she remembered the letter she had written to her children on Mother's Day this year.

She decided to review it and knew it had been God's words that had been written through her hands. The following letter is what He had written to each of her children this year.

# Mother's Day Message

As I write to you God reminded me it is really the children's day because without you I would not be a mother. I was given the greatest gift when all four of you were given to me to call my children.

In my eyes you are flawless in every way. I see the inner depth of you and know the great calling each one of you have on your life. It is my calling to be your prayer warrior and counsel you with Godly wisdom when you ask me for counsel. There has not ever been a time that God has not moved on my heart to pray in a certain way for each of you and let me feel your hurts, disappointments, and yes, even your joys. What a privilege it is to be called your mother.

Count your blessings every day
And thank God for them.
Never forget where they come from
It is always from Him.

Just know when times are hard
And the road is rough,
His grace is sufficient
And his love is enough.

He longs to have you come
To Him on bended knees
For that is the way
He sets you free.

Ask to see the world
Through God's eyes above
Then peace will surround you
With His awesome love.

Because of each of you I have a joy and peace every day knowing that God is doing His great work in your lives. Just remember when you have different paths to choose from you should seek Godly counsel from many and make decisions based on God's guidance and not emotions. Ask for His wisdom in all that you do and you will never be disappointed on your decisions on which road to take.

You are my sunshine and encouragement to run the race of life with zest. We only run the race once so my desire is that each one of you runs with the wings of eagles and reach the mountaintop that has your name on it.

I write this to the beautiful jewels in my crown. You are the wind beneath my wings.

As Mercy read the words that God had inspired her to write to her children she suddenly saw what her calling was. She had been begging God to find her a job so she would have an income. Now she realized that God had always provided for her needs and she had not had any work in a year. He wanted her to be a prayer warrior for her children so He could use them to make changes in the world. She would never again ask him to give her a job. From now on she would trust Him to put her anywhere that He wanted her. She would never let a day go by without spending time in prayer for her children.

*"I will tell you now what your purpose is in life. You have kept asking me what you should do and said you no longer had any purpose in life. I gave you four children whom I have called to be leaders in the world. Their calling is great and they need your support and prayer at all times. Each one is in training with me and you are their cheerleader to encourage and lift up continually so they will complete their training for their calling by me."*

*"Now you know that I never placed you in a job for long because your calling was to counsel your children. I will more than meet your needs I will also give you the desires of your heart. Let me name a few. You desire to pay for each child's student loans because you could not pay for their education at the time. Your desire is granted and I will provide more than enough to pay off their loans and your loans, too. I now have the freedom to give into your hands because you have closed the door on everything in your past."*

*"Did I not tell you over two years ago that your home was paid for? You will see it happen sooner than you think. You asked me to uncover all deceit and anything hidden from the builders and the men who are mortgagers of your home. I will show Casey everything they have done to deceive you and take advantage of you. I will show him even this very day and I will give him my wisdom on how to bring justice from the wrongs they have committed against you. When they took advantage of you it was Satan trying to attack me. He always loses and this time it will be revealed to the world. The noose they have made for your neck will be used on them and they will be hanged with their own rope. The builder will not escape my justice either. There is a part of the law that I will show Casey that will find the builder guilty and he will pay the price I demand for his deceit. You are by far not the only one the builder has taken advantage of and used for his gain. He has tried to keep his deceptive practices hidden but I will uncover them and expose him to the world. Because he has not been exposed in the past he has become bold and arrogant. You have trusted in me and it will be through your faith that I will move and sentence him for his wrongs.*

*Although it is a company there is one man who designed the fraud he has used on many for his profit.*

*The attorney for the builder thinks he will win because he has told you that you must arbitrate and cannot have a court hearing. He is not aware of the written law I will show Casey that says differently. When he is told he is wrong fear will enter his heart because his bluff has not worked. The reason the attacks on you were so strong is because Satan knows he has been found out and that his time is up. Even now he is preparing to flee as the word is released by Casey's mouth. Rejoice that I am in control and I will bring justice to you quickly".*

The next day Casey called and said he had settled with the builder and a check would be sent to her soon. God's word was true and He had shown Casey how to settle the case that seemed impossible. She knew that soon it would come to pass that the house would be paid for in a way only God could perform.

To this point in her life she had appeared as a failure to everyone but her children. She had suffered poverty, abandonment, and abuse by many people she had known but her Daddy had never forsaken her. She knew what it was like to have nothing and she knew what it was like to have plenty. From now on she would be content with each day and what she was given for that day. The most important task she had now was to get the word out to God's people so they could know Him and the power of His presence.

She looked down at DJ the little beagle that had been given to her just a short time ago. He looked up at her and she knew he had been sent to be her closest friend. She picked him up and held him tightly and thanked God that he had sent someone to love her unconditionally. She knew that the Promised Land was near and she could hardly wait.

Mercy knew there was one more problem her Daddy wanted her to handle before she started providing a home for the homeless and needy.

She had a man who had been renting from her for over a year. He had begun to cause problems ever since she had rented the second bedroom to another man in June. Before the new man came Perry had been the only one in the house for weeks at a time. He had been enjoying the house to himself and did not like having someone move in on his territory. She asked her Daddy how to handle the situation and to tell her what Perry was trying to do.

*"If you will think back you will remember that Perry would call you in Brady and ask you when you would be coming to Austin. He had been letting his dog run throughout the house while you were away. He also went through all of your papers and in your closet. He began feeling as if he was the ruler of the house and he did not like you coming back and being in control. Satan is quick to place his workers in strategic places especially where I am welcome."*

*"When the new renter, Ted came to live in your home he was young and positive. Perry did not want him in the house so he began telling Ted that they could rent a place together because you did not pay the bills and the house could be foreclosed on at any time. Then when you got DJ he told Ted you let DJ go to the bathroom in the house because he knew Ted was very clean and neat."*

*"He had been building up his defense against you because he does not want you to raise his rent. If you do then he will have Ted convinced that he should move into another place with him. Perry must be removed from your home because he has been sent to stir up trouble. If you will notice he does not profess that I am God and he is greedy and selfish. He is the children's father in replica in your home. Satan has tried to make sure you are controlled by one of his followers no matter where you go."*

*"Listen to me and I will remove the ones that are not called by my name quickly. You will look and they will be gone. You must have Casey draw up a written rent agreement and have each tenant sign it. Perry will refuse and move out soon. I have a child that I want to bring to you but I can not do it until Perry has left".*

Mercy knew that she must take care of the situation soon.

She asked God to cover her home with protection while she went to work for Kent and Kim in Cleburne. She had told Perry about not being at home but she had told him that she would return on Saturday morning. She would have to come back early on Friday and surprise him. She could feel the anger and deception of the man she had been with in Brady and she felt his attacks in the spirit. This meant she would have to spend the night in prayer and warring in the spirit. She knew she must have God's wisdom to know how to handle this situation.

When she returned home she saw that Perry had been on her computer. He had removed all of his food from the refrigerator as if she might eat it. Then he showed up with a huge sack of dog food and a gate to keep DJ from the upstairs and told her she owed him twenty dollars.

She felt bombarded by attacks and went outside to sit with DJ. The tears started flowing down her face and she couldn't stop crying. She felt no hope even though God had given her promises of things to come. It seemed as if nothing ever changed and she just couldn't hang onto promises any longer.

*"I have not forsaken you my child. I see your pain and despair. I could bring you home to me now and deliver you from the trials of life. Do you want to leave now or keep going? You are at the edge of the Promised Land now and I will deliver you. You can come to me or enter into the land and walk in my blessings. I will not have you suffer any longer."*

*"By now you know that the world is asleep. Everyone is concerned only with his or her own problems of each day. So very few of my children have my heart of compassion for others. You feel rejected but remember that the world rejected my son and He was without sin. It will just be you and me that walk through each day. My grace is sufficient for you and it will never leave you. My angels are all around you and they will protect you at all times. Trust in me with all of your heart and lean not on your own understanding. I am about to reign on your desert and bring showers of joy. Your barren land will flourish and you will rejoice at my mercy in your life. It is sooner than you think so gird yourself up and see my glory appear."*

*"Now which do you choose? Do you want to give up and come home to me or enter the Promised Land I am about to give into your hands?"*

Mercy advertised on the Internet and a girl called to rent the room for six weeks. She needed a place to stay until she finished her job and moved to another town. Mercy told Perry the girl would be moving in and would be renting the other room.

She told him to keep the bathroom clean and he just exploded. She knew he would be looking for some place else to stay soon. Then she just wanted to spend time alone with her Daddy.

Mercy lay lifeless on the floor and could not speak. How could she choose anything other than to serve Him however He wanted her to do? She remembered that His word said that many are the problems of the righteous but the Lord will deliver him out of them all. She could only cry out for Him to help her and she knew that He would take care of her.

She felt desperate and called her oldest son. He did answer and she asked him if he would help her get a hood for her car. He told her the car wasn't worth repairing and it would just waste money to buy a hood. Then she asked him if he would help her get a car.

He told her he couldn't because then he would have to pay for his wife's mother's car and he had given them enough. Then he told her to look for a car and he would call her back.

The phone call never came and Mercy realized she should have never called him. Her Daddy had already told her that a stranger would give her a car and she had not listened. She felt so bad that she had not believed in a miracle that God had planned for her. The next day a man stopped her as she was driving and told her he had a hood to fit her car. He would even put it on for her and she could pay for it when she could. Then he said God would make a way for her because He always makes a way in our life.

She began praying for her oldest son and suddenly felt the burdens that he had been carrying for so long. They were so heavy he couldn't see anything going on around him. She waited for direction on how to pray for him and then God spoke to her.

*"He has been consumed by all of the ones around him that are trying to control his life. His wife has the right values but the loyalty she feels for her parents is causing her to put them first in her life. They expect everyone to take care of their needs and never consider the injustice they bring to their children. Justin has become the provider for them and they expect him to give without question. Their control has caused his wife to lose her respect and love for Justin and she no longer looks to him as her husband but as her means to satisfy her parents. She has taken away his role as the covering for his family and all respect for him has been lost. He must choose to regain his authority over his family or they will consume him."*

*"Pray for him and I will give him my wisdom to handle the situation. If she refuses to let him care for her my way then I will set him free from his bondage. Even now he is seeking me for answers and I will surely answer. Never think that he does not care for you. He has so many burdens and decisions to make there is not room at this time to look at where you are. He will soon be set free and become the*

*man that I have designed him to be so just continued to pray and I will guide him in the way he should go."*

Mercy was thankful of God's reassurance that He would take care of her son, but she didn't know what to do with her own life at this point. She wondered if she had told herself that her house was paid for because that is what she wanted to happen. If that were so, then how would she ever be sure she had heard her Daddy's voice when he talked to her?

She ran to her closet of prayer and began seeking His face. Tears of repentance began flowing down her face when she realized she had been trying to control her destiny by asking for things of the world. She was so ashamed that she had tried to cling to material things instead of spending time being used to touch others around her.

*"I have allowed the battles in your life to help you realized what is important. You had made a house more important than me and did not realize it at the time. You wanted to help the poor and you did although you did not realize it. Everyone who has lived at your house had been in need of a place to live. You have housed drug addicts, minorities, homosexuals, and many others in an attempt to allow me to touch their lives. You showed them love, understanding, and kindness that they needed in their lives."*

*"If I choose to move you somewhere else how can you say that I have not answered your prayers? The house you live in cannot witness to my children. I can place you in a shelter and you can still serve me. I will release you of the desire for material things and fill you with the desire to serve me any place that I lead you. Now that you have repented of wanting things in the world I can use you the way I want to and touch others with my love. It does not matter where you live or what people say because you do not answer to them, you only answer to me."*

Then peace consumed her and she was happy that she had Hope to drive. She didn't have to impress anyone and God would lead her by His spirit to the place that He had waiting for her. All fear left her and she no longer wondered where she should be or what she should do. She would take each day as it came and be led by His spirit. Then she realized that she had accepted whatever her Daddy had in store for her and He had already shown her the Promised Land. It was almost time to enter the place He had set as her destiny.

Mercy told Perry that God was the head of her house and she only answered to Him. She wanted Perry to understand that he could not control who she helped because those choices belonged to God. God was faithful to protect her and Perry moved out suddenly without any explanation.

Mercy started taking Trin to church but soon felt led to take her to the new church close by. When they walked into the doors she knew it was where they belonged to worship. The praise was pure and there was no demand for ten percent tithing or you were going to hell. For the first time in years she felt there were others who worshipped God with a pure heart with no thought of material gain. They believed that if you seek the kingdom of God first, then all other things would be added unto you. The church she had attended in Odessa had become a "name it and claim it" congregation and she knew it was not the way she wanted to live. She was so glad she had found a place to worship and grow in God's word.

Days and weeks passed as she spent hours in her prayer closet each day seeking God and giving thanks and praise. It was if she was being prepared for something new but she didn't know what it was.

One day she realized she began her prayer by asking her Daddy what He wanted her to do that day. In the past she had always began by asking Him to help her with her problems that she would always present before Him. It was now that she realized she was seeking the kingdom of God first and was not concerned with the issues in her life. When she did the Father's will he would take care of everything else without her having to remind Him. She was learning to put Him first above everything else in her life and was experiencing a peace she had never had before. His anointing was becoming stronger upon her and the cloak she had grown to love was not leaving when she left her prayer closet.

Every day Mercy began her day asking for her Daddy's perfect will and telling Him how much she loved Him. She began to long to tell her children what she had been through but she knew it was not yet time. God would do it His way and it would be perfect.

*"You now understand why you have undergone the trials of your life. I allowed you to be hungry to understand how the ones feel who have no food and they do not know to trust me. You have been without parents to understand the loneliness of the fatherless, and you have been poor to know the feeling of defeat by the ones who have nothing. You have learned to understand the loss of the widows and the persecution of those who thought you would not work. It has developed my compassion within your spirit so when I want to touch someone through you they will see that you are sincere in knowing where they are in life. Then I will speak through your lips and offer them the bread of life that is my love. You have been obedient without complaining and I have perfected my place in your heart as pure gold."*

*"Your children will know soon what I have been working on in your life and they will understand what I have done. When they see the revelation of my work in your life they will take the cloak of humility and clutch it tightly from that day forward. It will be at that time that they will truly understand how important the cloak is to all that know me. You gave them to me many years ago to be their Father so rejoice that I will do my perfect work in their lives."*

Gratefulness to her Daddy saturated Mercy's heart. She felt a new faith in Him that was so strong and sure. Doubt that God would never leave her was nowhere to be found and peace flooded her being. Her only desire was to serve Him and worship at His feet.

Mercy felt a compelling desire to pray for the father of her three children. She knelt down and asked her Jesus to pray the perfect prayer for his life through her. She didn't want him to sit alone day after day and not know the one who gives life fully. She knew that His presence could change any heart no matter how cold and hard it had become. She also knew that the time they had spent together had touched him. Although she knew they could never be together she wanted him to have the peace of God and know that he was loved by an unconditional loving Father who would breathe life into his dry bones. As she was praying for him she asked forgiveness for any wrong words or actions she had done to misrepresent her savior. The lingering question of should she have stayed and tried to help him would not leave her and she asked for the answer to that question.

*"I directed your path every step of the way. You were obedient and stayed as long has I wanted you to stay. He felt my presence in your life and saw your forgiving heart and he knew that you serve me. That is all that I wanted you to do and he had to see that the mental abuse he showed to you was not allowed by me. Go to a book that you brought back from Brady and look inside. You will find the answer to your question when you see what is inside."*

As Mercy opened one of the books she had brought home from Brady she saw the poem he had written to her one-day right before he left. It was then she knew that God had touched his life through her and she had done what He had asked her to do. Tears flowed down her cheeks as she read the poem. She had typed it and stored it in her computer before she left.

# Ron's Song

When we met at a very young age
We would laugh together
As we would run and play.
You would smile and hold my hand
As I told you how I would be
A famous, famous man.
Things like this you seem to understand.

But as we grew older
And more and more apart
It is sometimes a wonder
How I held your heart.

All these years later as I look into your eyes,
I see the love and goodness and know
Why God's angels fly.
As I watch our children
Who now run and play
I know love like ours will never die.

After reading the poem he had written just a few months ago she knew that she had touched his life and shown him God's love. From now on she could pray that he would seek the One who had given him life and loved him all those years that he thought he had been alone.

# The Annointing Of A Chosen One

Everything in Mercy's past had been settled. She had repented of all of the wrongs she had done and had forgiven everyone who had hurt her. With a sigh of relief she bowed down to worship the One who had set her free at last.

Suddenly she felt His presence and it was so breathtaking she trembled. It felt as if a light was shining through her and it brought a cleansing of her soul she had never had before. Then the wisdom of God filled Mercy, and with it was a peace that could not be described. She did not care about tomorrow she just wanted to worship at His feet. As time seemed to stand still she felt His love washing over her in waves. Then He spoke to her so tenderly that she dared not move.

*"You have crossed the finish line to your training and I have cleansed you and made you holy for my kingdom. It is time to anoint you to walk in my ways and be led by my spirit. If you will walk humbly with me and obey me the anointing will stay upon you. It is now time to pay your vows that you made to me many years ago. When you keep your vow I will keep mine and pour out my blessings upon you more than you can imagine."*

Mercy remembered then that years ago she had promised God that she would quit smoking if He would help her pay all of the debts that she owed. Over the years the debts had dwindled to almost nothing and she knew it was time to keep her word. She wanted to walk in His blessings and be led by His spirit so much that she would do it with the help of Christ.

It seemed as if she was in His presence and never left as the days went by. She was not moved by anything that came against her because she knew He would overcome any adversity.

She began taking Trin every Sunday to the church they had found called Point of Grace. The minute they walked in it felt like home to her. The worship was so pure and the teachings fed her soul that had been starved for many years. They didn't collect money to buy the pastor a new Mercedes like another church she had attended and they didn't teach that you had to give money and you would be blessed. Everyone had a genuine love that touched everyone they came into contact with. They believed that God answers prayer and they prayed for each other with their hearts instead of just with their mouth.

Everyone had threatened foreclosure on her home so any times she began to know they would not win. It seemed as if the enemy was so intense that all of those against her were fighting against each other. Her faith took on new strength and she began walking with a knowing that it was all in God's hands and he would take care of it completely.

Each day Mercy spent hours in the Master's presence and was saturated with His spirit. The anointing grew and she began to see the pain and brokenness in the lives of everyone she met. She had always thought that her life was a failure and that others around her had everything going for them. Now she realized that everyone had burdens and many were desperate to be set free. She understood that she was seeing the hearts of everyone through the eyes of God. His compassion filled her being and she could feel what a person was really feeling. The trembling never left her and she knew it was His holiness that covered her soul.

*"Now you know why I have never given up on my children. They don't understand how badly I long to set them free from the bondages that keep them from me. Pride leads them to become self centered and greedy and it becomes an obsession that is never satisfied. I need to touch many through you so that they will come to me and be set free. Their spirits have become broken and shattered. Many are on the verge of giving up and others plan suicide. It is Satan's way to destroy the work of the cross and giving up is his greatest tool to destroy my children. When my spirit is upon you it breaks the yolk of sin and I can reach out to those who are willing to hear my voice. I will begin to bless you and you will be a blessing to others as I reach out to them. The ones who gave up on you and said you could never do anything will be astonished at the change I am about to do in your life. It will be such a miracle they will believe the testimony that you will tell of my great mercy. The cloak of humility must never leave you and you will fulfill my greatest commandment, which is love. My love is pure and unconditional and they will know me through that love."*

*"I have allowed you to go through the strictest of training and walk through the valleys of pain and suffering to increase your faith in me. You will walk by faith and not by sight as you walk in my anointing and nothing shall be impossible as long as you trust in me. I have touched you and made you whole in your brokenness and that is what I long to do for all of my children. Begin to praise me as I start to pour out my blessings upon your life."*

Each day Mercy spent hours talking to her Daddy. He shared His deepest secrets with her and she realized that only the Ones that knew Him would believe what He had told her. Every morning when she woke up she began praising Him and she asked Him what He wanted to do with her that day. Her heart's desire was to do His will and walk in the anointing she loved so much.

As the days passed she began to understand that she had been led by God every step of the way. The loneliness and pain were no longer there. Everyone in church was caring and she was filled with peace. The sermons taught her in a new way and she realized that there were people who could love you just like you were. The greatest commandment is love and the ones in this church were truly serving God the way they should.

As the anointing increased her faith increased and she knew everything in her life was coming into place for the first time. As long as she kept her eyes on God he moved. When she even glanced at the world He stopped and waited for her to look at Him again. This had such a new meaning to her. He was her source and she could never allow herself to look to the world again for help. Then she noticed she was not trying to please anyone like she had done all of her life. Her only requirement was to please her Master and He would provide without her asking Him for help.

When there was no more of Mercy and she was filled with the Holy Spirit she began to realize how far she had come from the person she had been. She never wanted to go back to where she had come from. Goodness and mercy from God had covered her and she started seeing the world through the eyes of God. Everyone was hurting in some way and a great compassion for others began to fill her heart. Every experience she had been through had brought her to this place. She understood the ones who had no parents because she had none. She told them she had a beautiful father who led her minute by minute and loved her unconditionally.

She saw the little girl standing alone at school and understood because she had been that little girl once. She held the little girl and told her Jesus was her best friend and he was always there. He never made fun of her and would never leave her alone.

One day Mercy met a man who was so full of greed he was miserable. She looked into his eyes and saw his fear of loss. He had already lost what was important - his family, his friends, and even his health. She told him she knew where he could find the peace he had been searching for so long. It was in the presence of God and she would walk with him into the presence of God. He began to shake uncontrollably and slumped back into his chair. As they approached the throne of God he bowed down and began to worship. Mercy knew he had touched the hem of Christ's garment and he would be changed forever.

It was each day with her eyes on God that Mercy carried the anointing and saw lives changed. She began to understand the meaning of life. Each day should be handled so carefully as if it was the last one. As long as she listened and kept her eyes on God he moved through her. The joy of serving Him became so great she could see the very heart of God. She saw how He longed to touch his children and draw them to Him.

As she walked each day in the glory she saw the tenderness of God's heart. Every day she saw Him reach down and carefully begin to pick up the pieces of someone's broken heart and tenderly start putting the heart back together. His great love bound each piece to another piece and the new heart because beautiful works of art with no scars. The new heart had the heartbeat of God and it pounded with praise to the One who had been the mender.

*"Most of the time I will touch only one person through you at a time. It is a personal touch that will bring the reality of my existence that will never be forgotten. I confront sin and it scatters in fear when my presence is near. As we walk together you will understand why it is so important to realize you will have this day only once. You may never reach out and touch the ones that cross your path again and they may never meet me personally if you do not tell them who I am. I have so few that I can use to touch others and I need you to help me. I have placed my heart inside of you and have covered you with my spirit. Now you can see through my eyes and we will walk the rest of your journey together. You will understand why my chosen ones no longer care about the material things in this world. When you keep your eyes on me nothing else will matter. The secret*

*to peace is walking with me and having my presence. It is what everyone wants but they do not know how to find it. Help Me to show them who I am and how much I love them."*

Mercy was so amazed at the tenderness of God she could not move. How could anyone comprehend that God needed him or her? Then she was ashamed at all the days in her life that she had done her own thing and never once spent it walking with the One she loved so much. He had even sacrificed His only son because of His great love and she had given Him nothing but selfish requests. A burning desire raised within her to touch life every second and never miss a chance to honor Him. Once she surrendered to Him she never wanted to walk alone again. She felt the cloak of humility covering her and knew the world had to hear about the cloak that would change their life.

*"The world is moaning and grumbling loudly now that the wrong man has been chosen for president. They must know that I choose every leader. It is my world that I made and I am the Great King. I appoint other leaders under me to rule and I will rule through them. If they seem to be evil rulers I will cause good to come from their evilness. Did I not use Rachael to deliver my people from death? Xerxes was not a godly king but I used one of my children to change his mind.'*

*" This is the time for my people to pray and call upon my name. When they do I will hear them and draw their hearts back to me. They have drifted far away from me in search of wealth in the land of free flowing prosperity. Nothing is ever wasted by my hand. I will use this time of trouble to again become real to the world. Even now I am choosing the ones who will follow me to lead the world back to worship in my holy place. Those who will not bow to me will lose the chance of eternal life. Trust in me and you will see the great works I have already begun to bring my children back to me. It is time to get busy and start reaching out to the world"."*

Mercy began to understand that when others were rude or said hurting things it was because they were the ones that were hurting on the inside and wanted someone to help them. The first instinct was to get mad and tell someone how he or she was mistreated. She was now learning to pray for those that hurt her and persecuted her. When she prayed for them then God went to them and confronted them. It was an act of forgiveness on her part and any bondage of guilt was broken from her life. It sounded so easy but doing it was harder. Walking by faith meant walking alone with God and believing that He was there when she did not feel Him or hear Him. Her spiritual eyes were opening and faith grew as she kept walking. She had given herself away as a little child and her Daddy was carrying her in her helplessness. By faith some days He carried her and some days He walked with her.

One day Ashley lost her patience with Trin and Mercy saw the pain on Trin's face. She was so defenseless and hurt. The depth of her pain covered Mercy as she gathered Trin into her arms. She told Trin that Jesus was always with her and his love always covered her. Then she told her even when she could not be with her she would always be in her heart. As she touched Trin's tiny heart with her hand she felt God's hand on hers and knew He would always cover her with His love. How amazing was the love of God that could look down and cover the pain of a small child. Yet she was a small child in His sight and she walked in His love.

*"You saw how much it moved you to see Trin hurting. That is how I feel when you hurt. Run to me and I will take your hurt and pain and replace it with my love and peace. I am everlasting and I do not change or ever quit loving you. Trin will see your faith and she will learn to walk in greater faith than you do. She will never forget your words or the touch of my hand this day so rejoice. Her pain will become beauty marks in her life that will touch many in the world. I have made her bold to carry my word and to believe in me. She prays to me often and I hear her every cry. You were that little girl years ago and I never left you. I will never leave her and she will walk in my blessings all the days of her life. She may not*

*even have her own bed to sleep on today but I will give her spiritual blessings that are the real meaning of life. You are her safe place and I will help you train her in the way to go. She will be a great blessing to many and a light to the ones that are hurting."*

The promise God gave her caused Mercy to see her fragileness. He had promised to bless and walk with the tiny child she cherished so much. The gratefulness in her heart exploded as she realized just how much her Daddy really loved her. That awesome love covered all of the loneliness she had felt since her mother died. His plan for her life was unfolding and it would touch the lives of many one person at a time. If only she could tell others how important it is to teach the children from birth about His awesome love. Greed would have to leave and all eyes would look to Him instead of the world.

As Mercy began each day she started seeing through the spiritual eyes of God. The true meaning of life unfolded and she knew what life's journey meant. The most important things were relationships that gave unconditional love to everyone. Everyone she met had a broken heart from the disappointments and hardships in life. She started smiling at everyone she met no matter how she felt and she noticed others smiling back at her. Then she started encouraging everyone she talked with to thank God for every blessing He had given to him or her.

Each day she touched one person at a time and the anointing grew stronger. She remembered that someone had told her to give what you have needed of and God will supply your needs. Nothing she gave was material but the spiritual gifts she offered breathed life into every person she touched. Encouraging others became a way of life for her and the pain from her past was gone.

*"I reach out through you one person at a time. Sometimes you feel that your efforts are in vain but I assure you they have touched many that you don't even know. The ones you touch will touch others and my love will spread throughout the world. Love is my*

*greatest commandment because it covers a multitude of sins and heals all wrongs. My children must learn that is not what they own it is whom they serve that directs their life. I have chosen you to counsel your children because they have been chosen to be my leaders. You will counsel and pray for them as I direct you for their strength and perseverance. Your calling is even greater than theirs because they are still learning to listen to me and you hear me and obey. Count it all joy for the trials all around you for they are the perfecting of your faith. My plans are perfect so you must walk by faith and not by what you see."*

There was something Mercy had wanted to do for a long time. She decided to invite her sister's four boys to her home Thanksgiving weekend. They had no family and she was ashamed because she had not contacted them in years. They were all close to her age and she had been very close to them when she was a child. It would be a time to encourage them and love them with God's love.

All four boys came to dinner on Saturday after Thanksgiving. Everyone reminisced the past and shared their failures and successes. Mercy was the only one left from their extended family. She vowed she would pray for them everyday and share God's love with them. Everyone was in agreement that spending time with family is one of the most important times in life.

Every day one of her children called Mercy for counsel. She prayed for hours to let her Daddy speak through her mouth. Then one morning Ash came by to get an insurance card and as Mercy looked for the card in her desk she found an old e-mail. She had received it from a friend two years ago and she had kept it to share with others. It saddened her that she had filed it away and not shared it with others. It was about a 17 year old boy who had written an essay for his class. The subject was what heaven was like and it was the last thing he had ever written. He told his parents it was the best thing he had ever written and they were excited but never read it at the time. Little did they know it would be the last thing he would ever put in writing.

Their son died just a few months later. He was driving home from a friend's house when his car went off of the road and struck a utility pole. He emerged from the wreck unharmed but stepped on a downed power line and was electrocuted.

His parents were in shock and wanted every thing he had done in school so they sent a cousin to clean out his locker at school. In the locker was the essay he had handwritten. As his parents read the essay they were so moved by his words they asked everyone they knew to share his essay with others. It would be their son's way to witness even while he was in heaven. Peace filled their souls as they shared because they knew he had been ready when God took him to his heavenly home.

David's essay: The Room...

In that place between wakefulness and dreams, I found myself in the room. There were no distinguishing features except for the one wall covered with small index card files. They were like the ones in libraries that list titles by author or subject in alphabetical order. But these files, which stretched from floor to ceiling and seemingly endless in either direction, had very different headings. As I drew near the wall of files, the first to catch my attention was the one that read "Girls I have liked". I opened it and began flipping through the cards. I quickly shut it, shocked to realize that I recognized the names written on each one. And then, without being told, I knew exactly where I was.

This lifeless room with its small files was a crude catalog system for my life. Here were written the actions of my every moment, big and small, in a detail my memory couldn't match. A sense of wonder and curiosity, coupled with horror, stirred within me as I began randomly opening files and exploring their content. Some brought joy and sweet memories; others a sense of shame and regret so intense that I would look over my shoulder to see if anyone was watching.

A file named "friends" was next to the one marked "friends I have betrayed". The titles ranged from the mundane to the outright weird "books I have read," Lies I have told," Comfort I have given," "jokes I have laughed at." Some were almost hilarious like "things I have yelled at my brothers." Others were ones I was ashamed of such as" things I have done in my anger" and "things I have muttered under my breath at my parents." I never ceased to be surprised by the contents.

Often there were many more cards than I expected. Sometimes fewer than I had hoped. I was overwhelmed by the events of my life. Could it be possible that I had the time in my years to fill each of these thousands or even millions of cards? But each card confirmed this truth. Each was written in my own handwriting. Each signed with my signature.

When I pulled out the file "TV shows I have watched", I realized the files grew to contain their contents. The cards were packed tightly and yet after two or three yards, I hadn't found the end of the file. I shut it, shamed, not so much by the quality of shows but more by the vast time I knew that file represented.

When I came to the file marked "lustful thoughts," I felt a chill run through my body. I pulled the file out only an inch, not willing to test its size and drew out a card. I shuddered at its detailed content.

I felt sick to think that such a moment had been recorded. An almost animal rage broke on me. One thought dominated my mind: No one must ever see these cards! No one must ever see this room! I have to destroy them. In insane frenzy I yanked the file out. Its size didn't matter now. I had to empty it and burn the cards. But as I took it at one end and began pounding it on the floor, I could not dislodge a single card. I became desperate and pulled out a card, only to find it as strong as steel when I tried to tear it.

Defeated and utterly helpless, I returned the file to its slot. Leaning my forehead against the wall, I let out a long, self-pitying sigh. And then I saw it...the title bore "People I have shared the Gospel with." The handle was brighter than those around it, newer, almost unused. I pulled on its handle and a small box not more than three inches long fell into my hands. I could count the cards it contained on one hand.

And then the tears came. I began to weep. Sobs so deep that they hurt. They started in my stomach and shook through me. I fell on my knees and cried. I cried out of shame, from the overwhelming shame of it all. The rows of file shelves swirled in my tear-filled eyes. No one must ever, ever know of this room. I must lock it up and hide the key. But then as I pushed away the tears, I saw Him.

No, please not Him. Not here. Oh, anyone but Jesus. I watched helplessly as He began to open the files and read the cards. I couldn't bear to watch His response. And in the moments I could bring myself to look at His face, I saw a sorrow deeper than my own.

He seemed to intuitively go to the worst boxes. Why did He have to read every one? Finally, He turned and looked at me from across the room. He looked at me with pity in His eyes. But this was a pity that didn't anger me. I dropped my head, covered my face with my hands and began to cry again. He walked over and put His arm around me. He could have said so many things. But He didn't say a word! He just cried with me.

Then He got up and walked back to the wall of files. Starting at one end of the room, He took out a file and, one by one, began to sign His name over mine on each card. "No!" I shouted as I pulled the card from Him. His name shouldn't be on these cards. But there it was, written in red so rich, so dark, and so alive. The name of Jesus covered mine. It was written with His blood. He gently took the card back. He smiled a sad smile and began to sign the cards. I don't think I will ever understand how He did it so quickly, but the next instant it seemed I heard Him close the last file and walk back to my side.

He placed His hand on my shoulder and said, *"it is finished".*

I stood up, and He led me out of the room. There was no lock on its door. There were still cards to be written.

Now Mercy understood why she had taken the journey with God through her life. There were so many things she repented of and many times she had cried when she realized the hurt she had caused others. In a whisper she asked her Daddy,

"Are the rooms in my heart clean yet?"

*"As we took the journey through your life His blood covered every thing you repented of and erased it from your life. There are still four rooms that we must visit before you begin counseling your children. Those rooms are the ones each child has occupied since birth. They are filled with love but also with painful scars you made upon each heart unknowingly. When we have finished cleaning those rooms and replacing the scars you have with beauty marks then I will represent you to each child so they will know your heart. Then they, too, will have beauty marks where their scars were and your family will be made whole. They will begin to trust you with all of their heart because they will recognize my voice coming from you. Are you ready to complete your healing?"*

Mercy took in a deep breath and bowed her head. She knew the pain might be great but she had to visit each room to be healed. More than anything she wanted her children healed from their past hurts so she knew she had no choice but to take this walk that was the most important.

When she entered the first room she saw Jesus standing by millions of cards with Justin's name on them. He had already signed each card with His nail-scarred hand and there was only one that had not been signed. It read "abandonment".

*"You ran away and left him in Odessa with the office the both of you had shared. You left without any warning. This caused him a lot of pain and hurt because he did not know how lonely you were there. You are forgiven and I will explain why you left. Then his heart will be healed and he will understand and forgive you."*

The tears flowed down Mercy's cheeks as she realized how terrible she had treated her son. Odessa had held a lifetime of failures and scars and she had left to be set free. Only Christ in His infinite wisdom could explain her heart to her son, but she knew He would.

The next room she entered also had millions of cards and they, too, had all been signed. There were not any that were left to settle and she knew her relationship with Kim had been healed and restored.

The next room was filled with so much love it engulfed her being. She felt sad there and she knew it was the loneliness Casey had felt while growing up. She asked Jesus to touch his heart and fill him with peace. His room had the spirit of Christ permeating her entire being. She knew that he had been chosen to serve her Daddy in high places that her family had never known. Integrity stood firm and dominant in the room and it covered his name with honor. She had never had a spiritual experience so great and it was breathtaking.

The last room held sadness and it broke Mercy's heart when she entered. One card was big and pain pierced her heart as she saw what it said. "Dominance and control over Ashley". When she saw what it said she fell to her knees and cried out for forgiveness. Then she asked Him to please set Ashley free of the bondage she had placed on her life so many years. She had only wanted to protect her but had never realized how she had held her captive for so long.

*"I have signed the card with my blood. She is now set free and I will go to her and explain that you never realized how you hurt her. I will draw you both close to each other and she will have a new freedom she has never known before. Encourage her daily and pray for her strength. She is a precious jewel that will soak up love as it is poured upon her. She will no longer be afraid to share her life with you for fear of rejection. Both of you will have beauty marks where the scars of life have been."*

Mercy felt a peace she had never known before as she left the last room. There was just one thing she must request from her Daddy. She asked Him to break the spirit of manipulation and control from Justin's life that had been transferred to him from his dad. She saw a pureness in his heart for God but she also saw another side of him that was dark and it lured him away many times. She was sure that he was not aware of the evilness that it held because for a few moments every now and then he would have a caring heart for her and his siblings. It never lasted long, though and he would be off to chase the wind for more money and power. It scared her at the hold it seemed to have on him and she begged her Daddy to please set him free. That same bondage had been on her life for years and it was just recently she had seen how bad it was.

She had married young and her husband had controlled her completely and convinced her that the way to be successful was to take anything you can get. She hated that concept and there was constant turmoil within her because she wanted to serve God more than she wanted to find "success", whatever that was. She knew God would restore Justin's heart to be a heart like Christ's and she committed to praying for him daily until it was finished. She was so thankful those evil spirits had not been transferred to Casey, but it was only because his dad had never lived with them or spent much time with him. She also knew he must be surrounded by Christians in his office to keep those spirits away. It didn't matter how long it took, she would stand and believe until her son was set free.

Her children came to visit for Ashley's graduation and she knew it would be a time when her Daddy would show her their needs for her to bring to Him.

She sensed a spirit of fear on Justin and she knew that it had come from Michelle's family. They had harassed him continually and she had tried every tactic to keep her hold on him. He did not know how to break that hold and was a hostage to their rampage. Mercy asked Kim to pray with her for his very life that Satan would love to destroy. They began a pray vigil and stood strong against the evil forces that did not want to leave. She realized how strong words spoken by others are and knew that it was a battle that was strong. As she prayed for Justin's eyes to be opened to see the truth she knew that he would begin to understand what was happening around him. She fasted for three days and prayed continually. At the end of the third day she felt the stronghold on his life was broken and knew she would see the evidence in his life.

As the attacks from Satan continued the accuser became louder through Michelle's sister, Janice. She seemed to have been the appointed one that taunted and tormented her own sister, Michelle. She called everyone she could contact and tried to find out every movement Justin had made. In the midst of her quest to destroy Justin she accused Mercy and her entire family of thinking they were God. Her outrage was unbelievable and Mercy spent hours daily praying for Janice's eyes to be opened to see the truth. Mercy was not sure how to pray for someone with such a twisted mind that was out of control.

*"The accuser speaks through anyone that will let him. Janice knows me but has been led astray by others around her. Confusion will take its place soon and she will become frustrated to the point she will pray. I will then show her my words that say not to judge others*

*unless you want me to judge you. I will also remind her not to cast the first stone unless she is without sin. I love her but she cannot hear my voice until she seeks me. When she is serious to find me then I will show her the truth. You must keep praying for her until she comes to me for answers. Do not judge her actions now or you will be out of my will. Every time you know she is gossiping lift her up to me and I will convict her heart until she cries out for my help. This is why I tell you to pray for those who persecute you because I will hear your prayer and touch her heart with my presence. Do not respond to anything she says but bring everything to me in prayer."*

*"Until now you have given all that you had to anyone that asked but there were times this was not for their good. When you give do so without expecting anything in return. Inquire of me and I will tell you if you should give when someone asks for something. Many times you have given to supply their wants instead of their needs and this is a dangerous act. Unknowingly others will look at you as their source instead of coming to me. You gave many times because you wanted to be loved. You must give to others what you have needed have and it will be returned to you in abundance. If you need love then love someone. True giving is giving to others to honor me. I will impress upon your heart when I want you to give to someone from this time forward. Love is the greatest gift you can ever give so begin to let it flow from you now."*

Beginning the very next day Mercy began spending each day thanking her Daddy and praising Him for His grace and mercy upon her life. When things seemed out of control and Satan began taunting her she started saying "Jesus". That one word held more power than any tactic Satan could use.

Soon another broken hearted person came to stay in God's house. His name was Paul and he was fighting alcoholism. Just days after he came Mercy's laptop computer disappeared and no one knew who toke it. It had the book she had spent months writing stored in it. It was not her place to judge Paul and accuse him of theft.

Mercy asked Paul about the computer and he said he might know someone who could have taken it. Later, he said the person didn't have her computer. Mercy took the matter to her Daddy in prayer.

*"What Satan tried to steal from you is not lost. He wants to keep my words from ever being read by others. I will have Casey email you the copy you sent him months ago and it will be published. It does not matter who took the computer. My words you have written will burn like fire in their minds when the read them and all will not be lost. I love to create miracles out of disaster and show off my glory. The world does not understand my ways so don't bother to make a big issue of the lost computer. Satan is a thief and he will be exposed in due time. Right now we must work diligently to touch all of my hurting children."*

A month later Paul said he would be moving in two weeks. Mercy reminded him that he should tell her who took her computer. He refused to respond and never spoke to her again. .

Every day Mercy prayed for Paul and she encouraged him not to drink. He went to AA and church and began to recover from his addiction. Then one Sunday he left for church and never returned to take anything that belonged to him.

Mercy met Darla just before Paul disappeared. She had replacements on both knees and her hip was out of joint. She was an alcoholic and cursed with every breath. She told Mercy that God had brought her from Wisconsin to start a new life.

Darla and Mercy became friends and she became the next one to live in the house that God had provided for his abandoned children. Mercy prayed for her daily and encouraged her to trust in God for everything. Darla started reading the bible and God began moving in her life.

Touching others and making a difference in their life was the reason Mercy lived each day to the fullest. Her greatest joy in life was to see the hand of God reach down and touch someone who had lost hope.

There would be many that would be sent to Mercy in the years to come. She knew that most of them would be lost to the world if she didn't reach out and touch them. It did not matter to her that no one understood her mission. Her only calling was to serve her Daddy no matter what He asked her to do.

Out of nowhere Mercy sensed a miracle was coming her way and she did not know what it was. Then her Daddy came and talked with her.

*"It is time to send this story to the publisher so that it can reach my children and change their hearts that are cold. I will lead you where to go to get these words published and it is time for the miracles to come into your life. It is now time for me to move the mountains that you have faced for years. Rejoice and praise me as I move quickly and perform my miracles."*

As His presence consumed her very being she felt the comfort of the cloak she had been wearing for so long now. It had become such a part of her she rarely noticed its presence. It was the cloak of humility that had given her hope when everything seemed impossible. More importantly, her hope was in God and nothing else mattered. The material things of the world no longer caught her attention and she never even wondered how much money she had at any given time because she knew that He would supply her needs at just the right time.

Most of the time He supplied her needs without money. He helped her through others as she concentrated on serving Him with all of her heart. Only by wearing the cloak did she walk with Him in peace as His love flowed from her to everyone around her. The secret to life was walking humbly with her God in total surrender to Him. As she looked closer at the cloak she saw His love had saturated her and His peace covered the love as it flowed like a river producing life to the fullest. Then she remembered she had asked her Daddy to help her live life to the fullest and she realized she was doing just that. There was no prayer left to pray except to praise Him for His presence. It was in His presence that she had the fullness of life and that is all she needed to serve Him.

*"I want you to be my example of what life is meant to be for my children. The world is desperate to find help but everyone looks in the wrong places. All I require is that they come to me with a humble heart and spend time with me. I will do all of the rest for them. They have become blinded by the glitter of what money can buy and when the money is no longer there then they panic. Until now money has been their god because it has flowed freely and in abundance. I will remove their god and they will have to choose whom they will serve. When they see your peace they will want what you have not knowing it is free from Me to those who are willing to let Me be their God. I will speak through your mouth and love through your heart so they will know me and be set free. Trust Me in this and believe what I am telling you for I will bring it to pass quickly."*

# The Promised Land Is Real

There he was in the distance. She recognized him immediately although she had never met him face to face. Her eyes caught his and time stood still. It seemed like forever as they looked into each other's eyes and understood what was taking place. He walked slowly toward her and she thought she was going to faint. He was the one her Daddy had told her would be her soul mate and he was gorgeous. His eyes were deep as velvet yet sparkled like the sun. She knew God always kept His promises but it was coming to pass all that He had spoken and it was breathtaking. It was such a beautiful moment she couldn't move. It felt like time was standing still.

He approached her and held out his hand. They both knew this was the time they had waited for all of their lives. He told her that he had wanted to meet her for eight years and thought it would never happen. She looked into his eyes and knew he was the one God had told her about only a short time ago. She had seen his face many times as she wondered how she would ever get to meet him. He was so alive and full of confidence. He told her that the book she had sent him years ago had changed his life. Now when someone stood before him he could see into the depths of their heart. God had taught him to look at the intent of the heart of man and not judge his actions alone. He had been appointed by God to be a righteous judge and was learning to walk in his ways.

Mercy trembled as she realized the amazing miracle God had done because she had been obedient to send a book to a stranger. When she had mailed it she became afraid that the courts would put her in jail for harassment. Two days later she was in line at the bank and suddenly she began weeping. She saw the man she had mailed the book to on his knees praying and she knew he had read the message she had sent him. She had marked the pages about God choosing righteous judges to judge His people that judged the heart and not their deeds. Then she knew she had been used of God to reach a man in authority in the most unusual way.

For the next eight years he had grown in learning how to judge in a righteous way instead of the worldly way. At the time she had sent the book she had been embarrassed but now she was glad she had been obedient.

She had never forgotten his name. Without thinking she chose to call him Daniel. He had sent her a Christian card and told her that her son was amazing and he would reach the mountaintop and look down on us. He knew both of her sons' destinies just like she knew it. Someday Casey would be a Supreme Court justice and he would be the best one that had ever served. She also knew that Justin would be a federal judge and a righteous one. Right now she just wanted to get to know someone that God loved so much.

They had been together less than five minutes but the bond was so strong she knew it came from God's hands. Daniel looked so young she wondered if he was too old for her but then decided that was not her problem. Her heart was young and so was her mind. She immediately loved his positive attitude and sincere kindness. She knew why he had been chosen to judge God's people. Her Daddy had truly saved the best for last in her life.

*"You waited all of your life for someone to share your life with. Remember all of the times you told me that you wanted a man who would love you with all of his heart? You asked for someone that would cherish you and not want to own you and control you. He has also wanted a woman all of his life who would love him for who he is and not what he has accomplished. He wanted someone who didn't care about the power and position he holds but a woman who loved his spirit man. He listens to my voice and I told him that you were that woman when he saw you across the room. This is the perfect time to bind your hearts together. I couldn't do it sooner for many reasons. The ones in your past that I used you to touch would not have been in reach if you had been with Daniel."*

*"From now on you will be touching the lives of the elite and wealthy that think they have all of the answers. When they see your gentleness and purity it will touch their hearts and they will listen to the words that I speak through your lips. They will accept you because Daniel is respected and honored by everyone. He speaks the truth and takes no part of deception or manipulation. He sees these qualities in Casey and will be sure to help place him where I want him to be in my service. Do not be afraid of the different style of life I have taken you to live in. I have polished you and you can easily sit with kings and queens. This is because you have learned to look at a person's heart and not their outward appearance or position in life. You don't see the difference between the president and the homeless man on the street because you know I love them both the same. You will enjoy this walk in life the most and it will be full of joy and peace."*

As Daniel was talking to someone next to them she thought about the many blessings she had just recently received from her Daddy.

Of all the people in the world who knew her it was her little brother who had brought her his truck to drive. He had looked at her car and shook his head in disbelief that her entire family had asked her to drive all over Texas but not once checked to see if the car would make it. The car had everything on it worn out but by the grace of God she had driven thousands of miles to please her children. The radiator was leaking badly and the hoses were worn out. No one had even lifted the hood to see if it was in good shape. That was all right though because God had made it run to take her all of the places she needed to go.

She had given up the chance to find work to help her children and they never saw her problems. She would drive in the heat of the summer with no air conditioner and never said a word because she knew God was faithful and He would help her when it was time. There was a reason for her to suffer these things. Now she knew how the poor woman felt who had no one to help her when her car broke down. She always said a prayer when she saw someone broke down on the road because she knew what he or she was feeling. Mercy felt sadness for the man she had tried to help that was the father of her three children. As hard as she tried she could not understand how he could profess that he loved her and send her off in danger. She knew now why God had removed her from his life. He would have never taken care of her. Not only that, but he would have told her everything she had ever done wrong every day she was with him. He was out of her life now and she would leave him in God's hands. It was her time to experience the love she had always wanted but had never had.

Mercy felt so sad that no one who knew her had felt moved by her situation. She knew they prayed occasionally at night for God to take care of her. Did they not realize that He takes care of His children through others that will obey Him?

It was a stranger who met her at the store one day. He saw her putting gas in the little worn out car and radiance was shining from her countenance. She had just spent hours before her Master and His glory was still shining upon her. He heard God tell him to give this woman a new car and he didn't know what to do. God told him three times to go to her and tell her that God wanted her to have a new car. Finally, the third time God spoke to his heart he obeyed and walked over to Mercy. The words spilled out of his mouth and he was shaking. Mercy knew that only God could have a stranger walk up to her and give her a new car and all she could do was praise God. It wasn't just any car. The man had been richly blessed during his lifetime and he took her to a dealership in Georgetown. She found the silver car that God had promised her weeks before. It was a miracle. The man paid for the car and then he asked if he could pray for her. He prayed that she would be blessed all the days of her life beyond all comparison. Then he thanked God for choosing him to bless Mercy. Mercy cried and was in awe that there was someone who obeyed God no matter what He asked of him. She wanted to be as obedient and be used to touch others lives like this man had touched hers. She knew that this was the only way God could bless her and supply her need because anyone that knew her would take the credit for helping her.

*"You are learning my ways child. You understand that I had to bless you through a stranger. If it had been anyone that knew you they would boast and say they took care of you because you were helpless. It is my glory and I will not share it with anyone. You have been in the hardest of training for many years to become humble and not touch my glory. You have learned to be a blessing and leave the rest to me. You have learned my ways and the power of my resurrection. Most of all, worldly things do not hold your heart. They are blessings that you are grateful for but the love of your life is to serve me. Everything I have allowed in your life was for a purpose. I wanted you to relate to the ones I long to touch. I want you to help the poor, fatherless, and widows. Help the mothers with children whose fathers have abandoned them. I want to pour out my love and kindness to them through you."*

*"You have learned to be content with where ever I place you and now I can trust you to be used by me. The wealthy and famous that you will now touch would have ripped you to shreds before I trained you. They are full of fear and loneliness because they are scared they will only be liked because of their riches. When they see that*

*what they own does not impress you then they will want the peace that you have. Do you not find it amazing that they want what you have and you have had only me for many years? Material things will never lure you because you know my greatness and love. You can't look back at what might have been. There was only so much you could do to touch the ones in your past and the rest is left to me. Just pray for those who used you and mocked you and I will honor your prayers. Don't give up praying for them and there will come a day when they begin to see the true meaning of life by watching the miracles I have done in your life."*

Mercy looked at Daniel and he was still talking to the man near him. He was being so patient with the man but she knew he just wanted to spend time with her and share all the things they had experienced in life. She could tell that he would not show favor to the rich or famous. Until now the only person she had never known that had integrity was her son Casey. She knew Daniel had that integrity and never compromised it in any situation. He would be the one God used to counsel Casey and open the doors to his destiny. His reputation was impeccable and when he spoke everyone listened to his words.

Daniel came to her side and began talking to her. He thanked her for the book she had sent years before. He told her he knew God had to have told her to send it because his life had been changed completely. As he told her about the day he had finished reading the words she had highlighted that were meant for him a tear slid down her cheek. She asked him what day that was and he said it was October 17$^{th}$. She asked him what time and he said it was 11:30 AM. She knew that was the exact time she had been at the bank and knew he was on his knees praying. She told him that God had showed her that exact time and what was happening in his life. With his eyes watering he shook his head in agreement knowing that only God could do such a miracle in his life.

As they talked about the events in their lives the last eight years they both knew that God had been preparing them for His service.

He had wanted to meet her so many times but didn't know how to approach her. She told him she had felt the same way. She knew they would meet but she didn't know how God would arrange it.

He told Mercy that he had judged the hardest of cases since God had touched his life. He face was shining as he told her how the wisdom of God would fall upon him each time he had to decide sentencing for someone's life. He could see into their very soul and know if they were truly repentant or not. Then God always whispered what the sentence should be for the one standing before him. He was saddened the most when he looked upon a heart and it was black with the evil clutches of Satan holding it hostage. These were the ones who had sold their soul to the devil and would not turn back to God. He said he actually felt God's sadness and loss as he was told the sentence to give to the ones who would not choose God to deliver them.

Then he told her about the ones who were repentant and wanted to change their lives. Many had come to him later and thanked him for giving them mercy. He always told them it was God's mercy because He cared for them. He knew he could never take credit or touch God's glory because he was a servant of God and thankful to be used by Him. When he said the name Mercy he realized that God had sent Mercy into his life to be a companion in serving Him. Together they knew they would be used to touch the lives of those who could never be reached by normal circumstances. It would take divine intervention to reach the ones who needed God so desperately. He had known for years that someday he would be Casey's mentor for the highest of appointments but he had never known how God would bring them together.

They spent hours that night sharing everything that had happened in their life. As they talked their hearts became bound together as one. Then her Daddy reminded her of what she had heard once about this kind of certainty that only comes once in a lifetime. It became late and they hated to part but Daniel had an important ruling early the next day so they agreed to meet again the next afternoon. Mercy handed him the book that God had written with her hands and told him to read it and see how greatly she had been taken care of all the days of her life. He looked at her and knew she was the one that had been promised to him. He could hardly wait to know her better because he could see the intent of her heart and it was to serve God no matter what the cost would be.

They spent every available moment together in the weeks to come. There was such tenderness in their relationship and they both knew it was the presence of God. He told her he wanted to invite all of her children to his home for dinner and to spend time with them. It was set for the following weekend. Everyone agreed to be at Daniel's home at 11:30 AM. They both chose the time because it was at that time Daniel committed his heart to be a righteous judge for God.

Each family showed up a few minutes apart. Justin and Sarah came first. As Mercy introduced them to Daniel he immediately saw their hearts and knew that God had chosen them. He told Justin that he would be a federal judge someday. Then he told him he must be mentored to learn how to be a righteous judge. He must also learn how to choose his assistants and others under his authority. It would mean spending much time in God's presence and wearing the cloak of humility. Justin was moved by these words and knew it was true. He was in awe at the wisdom and authority that Daniel used and knew he was a role model he wanted to be like.

Next Kent and Kim came and Daniel met them at the door. He spoke to them and told them they had been chosen to help the poor and medically needy who were helpless and unnoticed. They both knew this was true and vowed to each other they would allow God to take them anywhere He wanted them to go.

The doorbell rang again. It was Casey and Daniel's face lit up as he hugged him tightly. He saw the great calling on Casey's life immediately and was greatly moved by the anointing that was upon him. Immediately he saw the great destiny for Casey's life and he knew he had been appointed to be his mentor. He saw the integrity and pureness of his heart and knew he was a special chosen child of God. All he said to Casey was that he would mentor him and help place him where God had chosen for him to serve. Those words held so much meaning that was unspoken but known that there was no more that needed to be said. A bond of trust and loyalty between the two of them began at that moment and it would grow throughout the years. They both knew it and were grateful for the goodness of God.

Then Ashley and Zack showed up. When Daniel saw her he spoke to her with such gentleness. He told her she would help the poor and fatherless and would counsel them in the home that God had given her mother. It was the home that God had paid for to provide a place for those that were ignored by the world. He saw her heart had a special love for children and knew she would touch the fatherless like no one else could do. He also saw the special gift God had given her to know the hearts of others. He recognized it immediately because he also had the gift.

It was so amazing that each of Mercy's children had such a special calling on their life. Justin would touch the criminals, Kim and Kent would touch the poor and maimed, Casey would reach the wealthy and elite, and Ashley would touch the ones abandoned by the world. He knew he was to mentor each one as he was led by God to do.

There could not have been a more appropriate time to spend as a family than this special day. Each one gave thanks for the blessings in their life and the opportunity to serve the One who had given them life. As each one left they gave thanks for the unity of a family that they had never had before now.

When everyone was gone Daniel asked Mercy to tell him the story of Casey's life. He knew there was something so special and he wanted to know all about it.

Mercy closed her eyes as she began and the tears began rolling down her cheeks. She told him the day she found out she was pregnant was the day she received divorce papers in the mail. Her husband had gone before a judge and said she agreed and the judge had granted their divorce.

She went to an attorney and filed for the divorce to be stopped. She didn't want a child to be born without a father. The judge cancelled the divorce and her husband left with the woman he had just married in Mexico. They went to Louisiana and she never heard from him again until Casey was five months old. He never sent any money for support so she worked two jobs and paid for the doctor and hospital herself. While she was pregnant she would sit for hours praying and listening to Christian music. She prayed over Casey's life continually and knew that he was a special child who would be used greatly by God. He must have heard her praying because from the time he was born he was very loving and had always had a pure heart. His dad had never lived with Mercy since he left so Mercy asked God to please be a father to her children. God honored her prayer and he took care of them all of their lives. She was glad their real dad had not stayed because he could never have been the father to them that God was. When Casey was seven months old she went before the judge and finalized their divorce. She was not afraid because she knew that God was their father now and she trusted Him with all of her heart.

After she finished the story they sat in silence as God's presence filled the room. They both knew that God had taken something so bad and turned it into something so good it was amazing. Daniel began to realize the desert Mercy had traveled for thirty years in the sacrifice to train her children in the way they should go. He saw her heart and knew she was also a chosen child of God. She had been through training and now she was on the mountaintop ready to counsel God's hurting children. She had been trained to reach anyone she was sent to help. The intent of man's heart was the subject and only God's amazing love that was unconditional could make the intent pure.

Suddenly Mercy woke up and realized she had been dreaming. The dream was exactly what Ash had told her would happen in her life. She knew it was God confirming all the promises that He had made to her. She didn't know when the dream would be real but she knew that it would happen. She had never met the man in her dream before but she knew him and she knew that he was the one God had promised to send to her. She had never met the stranger who bought a car for her either but she saw his face and saw the place where she had met him.

Mercy knew she must keep close to God because He was the one that met all of her needs and had been her husband for thirty years. He told her that He had given her the dream to confirm to her that it would happen in His perfect timing. She knew there were things to take care of and settle and she didn't know what to do.

Her cousin Connie called her and asked if she would go with her to Kent and Kim's to have surgery on her eye. Mercy knew she should go so she spent some of her last few dollars on gas to get to Brady. When she got there she was so glad she had gone there. Connie's daughter Sherry was there, too, and they opened their hearts about everything in their lives. She saw Connie's heart and it belonged to God. She had been living by faith and trusting God for each day and all that came with that day. Their lives were almost identical. Both had lost their mothers at a young age and had entered a marriage that held pain and being unloved. They had been desperate for love so just one kind word occasionally helped them survive for years. Life had almost passed them by but they had never lost their faith.

As they talked about all the years they had been apart it was both sad and healing. They had married cousins who were just alike in their personalities. They had controlled everything so much that the joy of living had long disappeared in both of their lives. There had been a spirit of self-centeredness on both men's lives to the point that they had no conception of the meaning of love. Love was buying groceries and having a home to live in. Connie's husband had passed away and now she had a new freedom to serve God and she had been delivered of the control and manipulation that had been on her life for years. She had reached the Promised Land and her heart's desire was to serve the One who had delivered her and set her free. It was then that Mercy realized that she, too, was in the Promised Land and she would serve her Daddy with all of her heart. Her dream would someday be real in life and it had given her hope that God would provide for her without fail.

*"My children must wear the cloak to enter into my inner chambers. When they enter I examine the intent of their heart. If they are wearing the cloak they have already been cleansed of their sins so I can look upon their heart and know if they love me. If they love me they will take care of my children that need my help. They will not ask me to do for them but they will ask me what they can do to serve me. I gave you the dream to assure you that the Promised Land is real and I will bring the dream to life for you in my perfect timing. You must believe what I tell you and it will come to pass. The world will call it a daydream but you know it is I speaking reassurance to you. All I want you to do is praise me and love me because you know me and my faithfulness."*

Mercy asked her Daddy to please show her how a true husband was designed to be and not how she had experienced in her past. She had always thought they should cherish their wife, love them unconditionally, and care for them unlimitedly. She begged her Daddy to let her know if that was how a husband should be or if it was just a dream she had always wanted to be real.

One day she met a man that came up to her and began talking to her. He was not outstanding in looks but he had a very gentle spirit. His eyes were full of kindness and he listened to what she said as they talked to each other. She had never had a man pay any attention to what she said unless it was to criticize her in some way. He was a complete gentleman and respectful of her. Their friendship grew and she saw all of the qualities she had thought a man should have. She knew in her heart that he was not the one that would be her soul mate but he was the example of how a man should treat a woman. They became the closest of friends and he thought everything about her was just wonderful. He told her she was beautiful and his love as a friend was pure. He never manipulated her to get his way and he allowed her to be a free spirit that could do whatever she wanted to do without criticism. Her request to God had been answered in such a perfect way. She knew that her soul mate would be coming soon because she had seen someone that had the qualities of the man she had been waiting for all of her life. She had traveled her journey through the past and had been set free of all bondages that had held her down. Now she was free to love someone without reserve and any hang-ups she would have had before now.

God had led her through the journey of her life and she had been delivered of all chains and bondage from her past. She knew that now the final journey with her soul mate was here and it would be the best part of her life. God had saved the best for last and she knew everything would happen exactly like He had told her. The best part of it all was that she would be able to touch many lives and let them know how much God really loved them.

The woman that had been named Mercy felt a renewing of her spirit and she leaped with joy. She would run the race of life and touch everyone her Daddy sent her to help. There is nothing as great as the touch of mercy from God and He would use her to reach many of His children.

Then the strangest thing happened. God took the cup of tears that he had held all of the years of Mercy's life and poured them out upon her head. Immediately she saw the beauty marks of all of the battles she had faced in her life. Those beauty marks would be the reminder to Mercy that she was free to tell the world how wonderful her Daddy was and how He had blessed her twice as much in the ending of her life. She knew her Daddy had big plans to touch his hurting children. There would be many that would need the Father's touch and Mercy felt honored that she had been chosen to touch others.

Mercy looked at the book she had kept of prayer requests during the last two years. Every prayer had been answered. God had provided a home for her to counsel the hurting people that were lost in the world. She knew that He would take each diamond in the rough and polish it to pure gold. Her calling by God was great but the rewards for serving Him were greater.

She had seen many lives transformed by the Master's hand and longed to see more pass through her life. It was truly an honor to wear the cloak of humility that opened the door for her to walk with God the rest of her life.